A DISTANT SUMMER

Deborah Martin

To Leonie

who knows what it is to be jake.

With thanks to those who kept me writing:

Emma, Suzanne, Richard, Alice, Steve and Roberta

While characters in this book may echo real life, they are still only inventions and this story is purely fiction.

Copyright © Deborah Martin 2021

All rights reserved. No part of this publication can be reproduced or transmitted in any form or by any means without the prior consent of the author.

A DISTANT SUMMER

28 April 2018

Elizabeth found the box that would upend her life in a room at her parents' home she had not been in for years. The dismantled bunk beds her brothers slept in when they were children were stacked with cardboard boxes and plastic bags. The room had not been touched in the many years since Sam and John Jr left to create their own homes and families.

The ancient blue paint was peeling along a crack by the window. She twisted the rusted catch and pulled hard on the varnished wooden frame to let in some of the crisp spring air. Dust motes blew into a corner.

Her parents stored everything for them here, waiting for the items to be re-claimed by their wandering children. The room smelled of abandonment. It was the storeroom for the bags of fabric for her mother's sewing projects which were left after she died. Christmas decorations and lights filled one corner. Another was taken over by a toy garage with its collection of small cars.

She recognised a bookcase she left and never removed which now stored their old school reports and science fair projects. JJ's rock collection sat on a chest of drawers which was filled with their 4-H ribbons from the county fair.

Her father's death came unexpectedly. For three years after the death of her mother, she came to see him when she could, but travelling back to Indiana from Virginia took time and planning. Her visits were never often enough and then suddenly he was ill – a cancer which spread silently before making itself felt. There wasn't enough time for all the things she wanted to say or feel before the task of clearing the house.

John and Hazel Williams lived here for all their 68 married years. They had been lucky that the farm came up for sale just as they needed a home. The compact house expanded with their family, adding bedrooms and a large kitchen that in the 1960s felt modern and spacious and fully equipped but which now looked dated and lacking room for all the gadgets Elizabeth had in her own kitchen. She wondered what new owners would do with it: rip out the cupboards for new ones and replace the Formica with granite work surfaces?

It was, Elizabeth acknowledged to herself, still a solid house which had weathered the passing time. She could see the new homes which had sprouted along the road over the past few years. Some had gone for the fashionable double storey entrance on their oversized houses set on bare lots carved from fields. She hated the nakedness of the new lawns. It would take many long years before the trees grew to provide shade, structure and interest. She wondered how many of the residents would still be here when the trees were mature.

She glanced across at the huge hickory tree which still had a rope swing, with a board for a seat, hanging from it, waiting for the grandchildren to continue what their parents had left behind. She would miss its surfeit of nuts that were gathered and dispersed among family and friends. Her mother's favourite cake had been a moist sponge loaded with hickory nuts with a mellow brown sugar frosting. A tear tingled at the corner of her eye and she blinked it back.

The master bedroom moved downstairs as her parents aged and the upper floor of the farmhouse was given over to guests and storage of the hoarded remains of their family life. Elizabeth found the box buried under old erector kits, shell collections and her glamorous elderly doll with a wardrobe of clothes styled in the 1950s. She stroked the soft embroidered lid and was immediately taken back to 1968 with the first blue sheet of aerogram letter she pulled out.

It had been slit carefully at the sides where the gummed flap had been licked and folded around the sheet of paper to form an envelope. The tiny, ruler straight writing crammed the tissue thin paper with close lines and additions along the margins and even a final thought on the back of the envelope, as if it was not possible to contain all the news inside.

She smiled to herself, remembering the thrill of finding one of these letters amongst the fliers and junk in the mail box. That it had travelled thousands of miles from Singapore just for her was amazing, but that it was written by a *boy*, who *wanted* to write to her, had been even more incredible.

A photo slipped out of a fatter envelope as she handled it. This was her first photo of him. He kept asking for a photo of her but she held back, afraid to let him see her podgy frame and ordinary face. In return he sent photos, but never of himself. Instead she saw images from the newspaper or his school newsletter.

This small black and white fading picture was the first glimpse she had had. Elizabeth rubbed it lightly with her finger, remembering the day it arrived.

5 June 1968

She felt the brightness of the sun on her closed eyelids and knew it was late. A hint of summer warmth rolled in through the open window. The clock read 7.48. Then she remembered – summer vacation. No school. No bus to catch and for the first week she was allowed to sleep in: an annual tradition which started when she began school nine years ago. Lizzie dragged the pillow over her head, willing herself to go back to sleep.

The kids at high school had been crazy during the last week. The seniors had already left, including her brother, John Jr, leaving the school emptier and at the same time noisier as the remaining students seemed to expand into the space left behind. It wasn't a time for real work. Everyone was thinking of what they would be doing during the long, hot days ahead.

She had heard Eric Hayden and his buddy in the cafeteria at lunch on Friday talking about having a party on the following Friday. He was two years ahead of her but lived down their road and every once in a while would nod at her, acknowledging her existence. The boys were sniggering over their plans for a hayride and who would be coupled up during it.

"I'd like a go at Anna," Eric had leered. Lizzie was shocked by the mention of her best friend.

"Naw," the other boy (Lizzie wished she knew his name) countered. "You want to stick with the older ones – they know more." He laughed at his own joke.

"It's nothing I can't teach her," was the reply and both boys dissolved into more laughter.

Lizzie remembered she was going warn her friend on the bus home, but Johnny had borrowed the family car to pick her up from school. Mom thought he was being extra kind, but Lizzie knew it was just so he could show off his change of status to graduate. He surprised her though by suggesting that they go for a sundae at the drive-in, something he would never have done when he was still at school. He ordered her favourite, hot fudge with whipped cream and a cherry, without even asking. But just as they were settling in to eat, kids from Johnny's class arrived in three cars and the gang hunched together around the picnic tables leaving her to sit alone in the hot car for more than an hour until he had been ready to leave.

A faint fragrance of bacon mixed with sounds of a distant radio and the clatter of plates from the kitchen. There was a grumble from her stomach which decided it was fully awake. There'd be no more sleep now. She kicked back the light blanket, grabbed last night's clothes and staggered downstairs.

It was unusually quiet in the kitchen apart from the radio. Sammy (no, he wanted to be called Sam now, she reminded herself) had come back from his first year at college a couple of weeks ago and every morning he took them through another adventure that hadn't been written in the infrequent letters home. Johnny was always trying to interrupt and if he couldn't add a sentence, he would burp or grimace so that his presence was felt. Today, neither of them was talking. Her father sat silently munching his cereal and her mother stood over the stove, stirring the eggs.

The news bulletin cut through the silence. "Presidential candidate, Robert Kennedy, has been shot…."

A icy stillness swept through her. How could this happen again? She could remember when JFK had been killed and exactly where she was when she heard the news. Everyone remembered that day.

"He's been taken to the hospital where doctors have worked through the night to save his life."

The world was already upset enough. Just two months ago, riots erupted in cities after Martin Luther King Jr was assassinated. Night after night, televisions filled with riots of angry black crowds fighting police and setting fires. In France, students took to the streets in massive protests and thousands of poor were camping in Washington DC on the mall.

At school, they all argued over what was going wrong. Some kids wondered whether troops should be in Vietnam while others supported fighting to hold back the spread of communism.   There were so many arguments with no answers.

"Here we go again," said her mother, returning to the overcooked eggs and scooping them into a bowl for the table. A curl of smoke rose from the unreliable toaster and she flicked the release to take out the slightly charred bread.

Her father stretched out his thick reddened hand to take a slice of toast and scraped butter across it. His weathered face looked a little older suddenly, a little more tired.

"The back field up by the woods' ready for mowing," he said, wiping away the outside world and bringing them back into their own. "Should dry quickly."

Nothing would stop the yearly cycle of cutting, drying and baling hay. The summer months were measured by how efficiently the crops could be reared and harvested. It meant long days to circumvent capricious weather that could destroy a year's supply of cattle feed in an afternoon's hailstorm.

Johnny grabbed a fourth slice of toast before Sam could get it and covered it thickly with homemade strawberry jam from the last jar of the previous season. His 17 year old lanky frame was still growing. The dark spurts of hair above his lips were managed by an untrained razor and occasionally he appeared at the breakfast table with dabs of toilet paper still attached to the micro cuts.

Nearly two years older, Sam considered himself more worldly, having just returned from his first three terms of college. He gave Elizabeth a playful punch and passed her the cereal.

"I'll take that," he told his father and they organised the day's jobs between them.

Lizzie's mother still stood near the radio, listening for further news. She passed the plates into a sink of soapy water and mindlessly cleared the meal's debris from the Formica covered table.   Lizzie wondered if this was a chance to get away before her chores were handed out but her mother caught her just in time.

She was weeding in the vegetable garden under a warming sun, when she saw the US Mail truck pull up at the end of their lane by the mailbox. She had posted her last letter to her pen pal nearly three weeks ago. He could have written back. If he had, she wanted that letter before Johnny got it. Once, her brother sliced open an aerogramme and tried to read the cramped foreign writing. The angular letters were very different to the curvy American letters and Johnny gave up. She did not want him to try again.

Lizzie rushed through the last row of beans, hurriedly grabbing at the invading plants. A few flowering beans came out as well and she tried to ease these back into the row before they were seen.

The mailbox was crammed with a free farming newspaper wrapped around advertising fliers and bills with a core of handwritten envelopes. Even without the foreign stamps, she knew immediately the letter was Henry's. The address was written in purple with a variety of coloured pens used to add messages like 'STAY COOL' and 'SWAK'. It would be instant fodder for her brother's teasing and she folded it into the pocket of her shorts to save for later.

The news hung over lunch. Dad, Sam and Johnny returned from the fields hot and sweat covered. The temperature was still rising and a scalding afternoon was ahead of them.

Dad took a long drink of iced water and then bowed his head to pray for the meal to be blessed, just like every meal she had ever known. Lifting their heads, Sam and John Jr both reached for the fried chicken but a stern look from their mother made them pass the dish to let John Senior have the first selection.

Kennedy was still critical in the hospital. A Palestinian man had been arrested: Sirhan Sirhan. Five others were injured.

"How does this keep happening?" her father asked after a few mouthfuls of mashed potatoes and green beans frozen from last year's harvest. "You'd think there'd be better protection after King was killed and JFK."

"And we haven't even closed those cases yet," Sam put in, pumped with political studies from college. "King's killer hasn't been found yet. And look at JFK. The Warren Commission said Oswald shot him all by himself, but then he's killed, but his killer gets a new trial and dies before that. That all sounds really peculiar and you can see why some think it was a conspiracy."

"This isn't even connected to the negroes or the war!" Her father sighed.

"I think they want to be called 'blacks' now," Johnny threw in to show some political acumen.

"What are you?" Sam asked, "A black panther?"

"Foreigners," her father spewed, "they're always trying to change the way we live. Why don't they just leave us alone?"

The letter with the alien stamps burned in Lizzie's pocket.

"Maybe because we don't leave them alone," Sam tried to argue. "Kennedy backed Israel in the Six Day War. This guy comes from Palestine, which Israel took over."

"It's not right, he comes over here to murder."

"John," her mother inserted in the debate, " you didn't want Kennedy running for president anyway!"

Republican roots ran deep through the Midwest. Having just received backing from the California primary the night before, Robert Kennedy would have been the biggest Democratic challenger in the election in November.

"Yep," her dad said, loading a piece of cherry pie onto his plate, "they'll have a hard time finding someone strong enough to win now."

Later, after clearing the table, Lizzie got a chance to pull out the letter when her mother sat down in the shade to finish her latest borrowing from the library bookmobile which visited their small town every two weeks.

31 May 1968

Hey, Babe,

Hope you're having a great summer. My friends and I thought your trick on the science teacher was really FAB. Did anyone get in trouble? We tried hiding our teacher's lesson plans so we wouldn't have to do them. Turned out he had a copy anyway and the WHOLE class got detention!!! Course, the kids who weren't part of it weren't that happy about that.

Are you out of school yet? We have to keep on working right up until July and then we have end of year exams. I can tell you NO ONE likes those!! I am studying round the clock.

What are you doing for the summer? My parents have come up with some really cool *plans – they're moving us to England! Yeah, it was a surprise to my sister and me as well. Dad grew up there, but I've never been. My dad's got a new job back there and so we're all going.*

I have never been there, so it's going to be reallllly interesting. The land of the Beatles, Procol Harum, the Rolling Stones. I am SOOOOO excited. But also, I can admit, a little nervous about the whole move to another country, after all I've never been there. At least my school is based on the English system, so I won't have any problems fitting into that. But what do you think English kids are like?

I want to let my hair grow longer, like you see them there, but Dad isn't very happy about that. I am looking at all the pictures of the Beatles FANS now just to see what they are doing.

Sorry to keep going on, but it has been such a SHOCK! Just as soon as my exams are done, I have to help pack everything up and put it into a shipping container. That's going to take <u>weeks</u> to get there, so we will have to live out of our suitcases for a long time. It's hard to decide what to keep. My Mum says I have to clear out the rubbish. Don't worry, I have your letters safely stored away.

Anyway, there is another bit of BIG news. We may fly to England through the USA. If we do that, don't be surprised if I knock on your door! I would love to see your farm and where you live and meet your friends. What's the closest big airport to Indiana? Maybe we can go through there.

Until then, stay groovy. Watch out for the boys.

Your friend,
Henry

28 April 2018

    Elizabeth pulled off her reading glasses and smoothed out the paper. The lettering was cramped and difficult to read in a fading light. It was hard to follow the writing without the glasses, unlike when it first arrived fifty years before.

    She tried to recall what they had done to the science teacher, but it was lost among the events from her youth that were trampled into oblivion. It must have been some minor infraction: surely she would have remembered it otherwise, like the time Jerry Farr cut off a large piece of phosphorus and threw it onto a bowl of water. The explosive flames nearly caught the whole room on fire. No one forgot that. Someone always mentioned it at their occasional class reunions. But that was their last year at school and this letter arrived three years before, just at the end of their freshman year.

    The fear she had felt reading that letter stayed with her. She had desperately wanted this photo and, at the same time, was afraid to receive it. They had been pen pals for more than two years and she carefully avoided sending a photo of herself during that time. She was full of little excuses about a film needing to be developed, or photos not turning out or she just ignored it all together. With every letter, she had hoped to get a photo but Henry was as ready with excuses as she was. This photo broke the stalemate and meant she had to send one back.

She was glad that was 50 years ago. Today, she would have no excuse in hiding - with instant messages and digital photos there is no delay. The alternative then and now was to send a fake photo, but she was too honest for that. She had to own up to who she was.

She remembered pouring over this small, slightly blurry polaroid for hours, trying to pick out a clearer image. It was a photo of four of lads – the members of his band. The one on the right hand side was HIM. He was standing in profile, but she could see he was tall, fashionably thin with dark hair just edging over his ears. Of course, he was the apex of cool with his own teen rock band. He was everything she could have hoped for when she was 14, if she had been a golden Californian beach babe and not a podgy, boring farm girl from Indiana.

Elizabeth pushed back a white strand of hair with her brown speckled hand. School had been a social nightmare. Miniskirts were making their way inland from the trendier cities on the coasts and fashion dictated slim, long haired figures with shapely legs if you wanted to be stylish. Paisley was in, along with bright, clashing colours.

She looked down at the swollen feet and thick legs. They hadn't improved with age, but that no longer mattered. In 1968, it was the end of the world. She could never be in the 'pretty' cluster of girls in her year. They were destined to be voted most attractive and become cheerleaders or homecoming queen. She wasn't one of their sort of people.

But, when one of Henry's letter collages fell open when she dropped her book one day, homecoming queen-to-be Sally scooped it up. The graphic lettering and photos jumped off the page and she started reading it. Word spread and soon the others in her circle wanted to know about the mysterious 'Boy from the East' as he became to be known. She was in touching distance of popular and it was close enough.

"Mom," Elizabeth heard a call from downstairs, "I've got the dishes packed. Dad'll be back soon to load up. Where do you want the kitchen boxes?"

She slid the photo back into the envelope and returned the letter to the box. Memories could wait but the realtor was due in two days to value the farm and they wanted to clear as much as possible before then.

"Kiera, just wait for your father. You can't lift them in your condition," she shouted down the stairs. The pregnancy had been an easy one, but felt increasingly long. Elizabeth was excited to meet her first grandchild and she was glad there were only a few weeks left.

She put the box on her personal 'keep' pile and sighed as she looked back at the room. The window grated when she pushed it down before closing the door.

A car crunched along the gravel drive. Richard was back. He wanted to go to a diner for supper but Kiera was asking for Italian. She suddenly felt hungry.

5 June 1968

Her mother sat in her reading chair, a comfy worn fixture next to the window with a large footstool. A soft breeze blew across her taking the edge away from the day's rising heat. They could hear the tractor in the distance, running up and down the field. The radio played quietly but every time the music stopped, the book relaxed in her mother's hands and they both turned imperceptibly to listen for any update on the news.

Lizzie lay along the overstuffed couch, scouring each fragment of Henry's letter. Usually this was the bit she enjoyed most. At school, others would take the pages and laugh and try and work out the long sentences in the funny writing. But at home, she could savour the amount of effort that had gone into creating them, which had all been done for her.

The letters were sometimes works of art, with op art patterns and scraps of stories cut from newspapers and magazines. Others were crammed with long stories of life in Singapore, with time stolen from friends or study or sleep.

The photo of Henry's band was the most unexpected item in the envelope. She always asked him for one, but couldn't admit to anyone that she was scared to get one. She could see him in her mind, just like all the fictional characters created in novels. It was the summer for reading Jane Eyre and she knew exactly how Jane and her Master looked even though there were no illustrations in her book.

Henry would look nothing like anything she could dream – she was sure of that. And, if he did, she knew a photo of her would shock him into never writing again. She kept from sending a photo just to keep the correspondence going as long as possible, but now it would all come crashing to an end.

Lizzie eagerly scoured the image of the band and especially the figure labelled Henry. He was slightly turned away from the camera, so she could only see his profile. She wanted to poke him and get him to turn towards her. She stared, trying to re-focus it and imagine the rest of his face. Every gradation of the black and white image was burned into her memory, but the happiness in receiving it faded into fear as she wondered what he would think of her.

A sour sensation low in her stomach grew as she re-read the letter. She could send him a selectively posed photo which made her look better than she was, or at least show as little as possible. But if he came to visit, there would be no hiding the truth. He wouldn't see the girl who wrote funny letters and shared his secrets, he would see the frumpy, fat farm girl.

A twitching anxiety spread along her arms and she wrapped them around her stomach in an attempt to contain it. She closed her eyes and drew up her knees, trying to squeeze out the excess energy.

Another news report came on the radio and her mother dropped her book into her lap to listen. "Robert Kennedy remains in a critical condition in the hospital. The Senator was shot in the early hours of this morning just after he was confirmed as the winner of the Californian and South Dakota primaries. He received three gunshot wounds, one of them to the head."

"That's no change, then", her mother, comforted, turned back to her book.

"I'm going for a ride on my bike," Elizabeth replied as she stretched herself upright.

"Pretty hot for that."

"I know, but I just can't sit still with all that," Lizzie said nodding to the radio.

The bike was kept in a dusty corner of the hayloft. The upper barn was nearly empty of last year's crop but the smell of dried grass lay heavily in the air. Soon they would be bringing in fresh loads of hay and straw in readiness for another round of winter.

She wiped the seat and felt the tires to make sure they had enough air. On the long flat roads with miles between towns, transport was essential. Until she was old enough to drive, the bike was her independence to visit friends in Clarksburg three miles away.

The gravel road was rutted and pitted. She wove her way around the worst parts. The harsh winter cracked the surface and spring rains turned a passable route into a muddy quagmire. Sometimes the school bus could not get through because of snow and a couple of times in the lower sections, it had sunk deep into the mud and had to be towed out. During the summer the road would be scraped back to level, but today it was an obstacle course.

The heat pulsed red in her face as she came to the last half mile. The small corner store had a soda fountain and the thought of an ice cold root beer waiting there kept her going. She leaned the bike against a bench set at the central junction of the two main roads that ran through the town. She bounced up the steps of Harrisons Home Stores and felt the coolness of the shade on the wide porch. The radio in the store was set to the local station. Mr Harrison looked up as the overhead bell tinkled her arrival.

"Any more news?" It made Lizzie feel very grown-up to be asking about current events just like her parents would have done if they were there.

"No," Mr Harrison replied, "They're just waiting now."

He poured a root beer into a frosted glass which she gratefully rubbed across her face. She sat on the porch and counted the cars go by while she drank as slowly as she could. Ed Tucker nodded when he came up the path, unsure whether he should speak to someone in the class above his own. He was at an awkward age when girls were either ugly sisters or goddesses.

Lizzie felt his surveying glance and the pivot point when he decided not to speak as he entered the store. She looked down at her sweaty shirt over shorts pulled up from dimpled fleshy thighs and tugged the shorts down discretely. The remains in the glass taunted her as she counted the calories she had just drunk and she left it unfinished.

Her best friend, Anna, lived three streets away in a ranch style house with an expansive lawn. They had been together all through grade school, defending each other and fighting in turn over the years. They even survived moving up to high school, although changing social groups tugged them in different directions from time to time. Anna was one of the smart ones. She was headed for college and her homework was filled with algebra, chemistry and English essays.

Lizzie preferred art classes and taking French, although she never knew if the words she learned sounded authentic as her teacher was not a native French speaker either. Maybe, one day she would get to France and see if she had learned it well.

Anna's house had a wide shaded front porch, which was a perfect place to sit on a hot afternoon. Lizzie knocked on the door and waited for any sound from inside.

A car horn beeped behind her and she turned to see a 4 year old Rambler idling by the sidewalk with her Uncle Dan behind the wheel.

"Saw Anna an hour ago in Montgomery Wards," he offered. The store was in the county seat of Fenton, about 14 miles away. "Don't expect she'll be back for a while. She and her mom were clothes shopping, it looked like."

"Thanks." At least Lizzie knew not to wait.

"Was wondering if you could do me a favour, Lizzie," her uncle went on. "Think you could ask Anna to babysit for the wedding? I should've done it when I saw her but I didn't want to interrupt them shopping. Jackie figures Simon's too young to sit through it all and she could do with a day out before the little one arrives as well."

Her father's younger brother, Dan and his wife Jackie were expecting their second child in September. Simon was two years old and just as mischievous as his father. He had inherited the reddish blonde hair, green eyes and the strip of freckles over his nose from his father.

They were just three days away from her aunt Charlotte's wedding. The women in the family had been discussing the details for months while the men tried to ignore all the fuss. Her grandmother was especially pleased about the wedding as she thought Charlotte would never meet anyone. Aged 32, Charlotte had been placed on a spinster shelf and not expected to marry, but she surprised them the following year by announcing her engagement.

The wedding was being held at the church Lizzie had attended every Sunday since she was born. There were two churches and a chapel in the small town, but each of them was filled every week with the families who put on their Sunday best clothes and went to pray together. Not attending was viewed as nearly heathenistic and definitely anti-social.

The family's church was the Cornerstone Methodist, sitting one block from the main crossroad in the town and Harrison's store. Its brick frame had an obligatory spire with a bell that was rung twice at 11 on Sundays to bring in the congregation and very freely when someone got married. Grandpa Ernest had helped build the church as a brick carrier back in the 1920s. The only time he missed a service was when he was away on a rare vacation or when he was ill which happened even more infrequently.

Dan tried to stay away from church as much as possible, but a family wedding was a special occasion where no excuse was accepted. He had one suit that would have to be aired and tested for fit, while Jackie had been meeting for weeks with the other family women deciding who would be wearing what. Apart from the high school prom, the only place where Midwest women could glam up in formal dresses was at weddings. For them, it was an opportunity not to be missed.

Dan moulded his face into its most endearing and pleading expression. "I know it's a little last minute, but if I don't find a sitter, Jackie probably won't speak to me until the baby's born – and that'll just be to get a ride to the hospital!"

Lizzie could not help laughing. Her uncle was always funny – the joker in the family who was always playing a prank on someone.

"Not a problem. I'll call her tonight and ask," she promised before Dan shifted the gear lever into drive and headed down the street.

The ride home hit the peak of the afternoon heat. By the time she arrived, a torrent of sweat streamed down her back and the light cotton blouse clung to her shape. She was red faced and breathless when she threw herself down on the living room sofa.

The radio still played in the background. Her mother was picking her way through her card box of recipes deciding on the menu for supper.

"Still no change," she offered nodding to the radio, "although it doesn't sound good for Kennedy.

"Saw Dan in town," Lizzie told her mother while sipping iced water from a glass. "Just outside Anna's. He wants her to babysit on Saturday, but she wasn't there.

"Have you seen Jackie's dress?" Her mother then fell into discussing each of their dresses – a conversation which had been going for months. Lizzie had tried to lose 10 pounds so she could squeeze into a smaller size: there was a dotted organza dress, but it only went up to a 14. Unfortunately, there was always a slice of cake or a freshly baked cookie and the diet never got going.

After cooling down, Lizzie decided to call Anna to pass on her uncle's request for a babysitter. The telephone sat on a side desk in the heart of the house, where its ring could be heard from every corner. She picked up the heavy receiver and paused to listen. They had a party line of four households and sometimes she picked up in the middle of her neighbour's gossiping. Fortunately, it was silent and she dialled her friend's number.

"Dan said he saw you shopping. Did you get anything good?"

"Mom saw some summer dresses she liked, but then she wasn't sure where she'd wear them. There was a cool kaftan with a huge paisley print. That was about the most radical thing in the store, though," Anna sounded dejected by the lack of choice. "I did get some new shorts and a tank top, so I am ready for Eric's party on Friday. You going?"

"Wasn't on the invite list -- like some," Lizzie sadly had to admit. "Anyway, we've got the rehearsal dinner then so I couldn't have gone anyway. You'll just have to tell me all about it."

Lizzie wanted to warn her about what Eric had been saying, but her mother was nearby pretending not to listen. Mentioning a party without adult chaperones in the presence of a parent was breaking the teenage code. Instead of being merely excluded from the event, an infraction such as that could get her completely ostracised.

She would have to call Anna when her mother wasn't around. Lizzie also wanted to talk her about the letter in private. She didn't want her mother to know how scared she was--she'd think it was silly to worry about it. Anna would understand. This was something you could share with your best friend who always knew what to do. Lizzie promised to call her soon so they could make plans for the long summer.

Lizzie told her about Dan needing a babysitter. "If you're not too tired from Friday night," she chided.

"Not a problem," Anna replied, "I always need the cash and I think your uncle is fun. And Simon is sooooo cute."

Breakfast the next morning was sombre. Robert Kennedy died in the early hours and the news was filled with world leaders mourning his loss and plans for the funeral on Saturday. No one noticed as Lizzie moved the food around her plate that none of it went in her mouth.

"It's so unfair for Charlotte," her mother moaned. "It's the most important day in her life and everyone will be thinking of the funeral."

"Whatever will be, will be," her father replied quoting the popular Doris Day theme song as he tipped cereal into his bowl. "She can't change the wedding date, and the world isn't going to wait."

"At least they caught the guy who shot him," Sam put in. "They're still looking for King's killer."

"It'll be the death penalty for sure," her father scraped the last milk from the bowl before reaching for the plate of pancakes.

29 May 2018

Elizabeth sank into the garden chair on the patio of her home in Manassas, Virginia, and put the glass of chilled pinot grigio on the table beside her. It felt good to stop for a moment after the busy weekend. Kiera and Dave had come from Richmond to stay with them over the Memorial Day holiday.

Richard hauled out the barbecue for the first grilling of the season and they sat for the whole day immobilised by each wince and sigh of their tiny new granddaughter, Zoe.

"I wish your grandfather had seen her before he died," Elizabeth told Kiera while gently stroking the newborn's soft head.

"I wish I could have helped you more with the clear out."

"Whatever will be, will be," Elizabeth quoted her father. "Anyway, next time I'll meet up with Sam and JJ and we will finish it off together."

The young parents left at the end of the afternoon, leaving an absence that filled the house. Elizabeth cradled the drink to her mouth and took a sip slowly, allowing it to linger in her mouth. She poked her tablet into life and searched through the headlines on a news website before one caught her attention: 'Robert Kennedy Jr calls for new investigation into his father's death.'

It had been 50 years and for most of that time she had not thought about the assassination or the killer, Sirhan Sirhan. Could he still be alive? Surely, with a crime so momentous, he would have been executed. She read through the article to discover he was still in prison and Robert Jr had been to see him. Having reviewed the autopsy and other evidence and talked with convicted killer, Bobby Kennedy's son believed the case was not solved.

"It'll be something for the conspiracy theorists to get their teeth into," Richard said, reading over her shoulder. "I'm not sure anything can be proved one way or the other after this long a time. But if he's innocent, it's a long time to spend in jail."

"It's a long time to still not know what happened to your father, as well."

Elizabeth had time to prepare for her father's death from cancer. Over the last six months of his life, she and her brothers had watched the decline. Their once robust and strong father melted into a delicate frame that had trouble standing. They couldn't stop it, but they were ready for the outcome. No one is ever ready for murder. She was 14 when Kennedy was killed – and so was Robert Jr. She shuddered wondering how she would have coped if it had been her.

For 50 years, the facts of that summer had been settled and built into history, but now one of the bricks had been loosened and no one knew what effect that could have.

10 June 1968

Hey Babe,

I've only got a little spare time – we're in the middle of exams and you know how I love to study!!! Just got to get through these so I am ready for our move to England. I was hoping we would be moving to LONDON. Carnaby Street would be really groovy. It's where it's all HAPPENING. WAY OUT, as they say! Can't wait to see it, but my Dad says we'll be living somewhere further north, a city called Leeds. Doesn't sound as exciting, but still it is a whole new country for me.
 I saw all about Kennedy's funeral on the news. I was AMAZED by all those people waiting by the side of the railway tracks for his body to go by. WOW that was incredible. Did you see it live as it happened? Because of the time difference, I was in bed and didn't see it until later.
 But, you said the wedding was on that Saturday as well? I am sorry- it must have been overshadowed by the funeral, or did you just ignore all of that? I think the rest of the WHOLE world was watching that. Can't believe your country had another assassination. Thought that was just in tin pot dictatorships!!!! Guess not, but then people are protesting all over the place.
 My Dad is worried about Susan going off to university in England. He is worried about her getting hurt after all the violence. We've heard about so many student protests all over the place. They

were against the War in London. I read that they were fighting with the police outside the American embassy. And now, it's the FRENCH students who are demonstrating and holding sit-ins!!

Do you get caught in any of the protests? You said there were riots after Martin Luther King was killed – how far away are you from the cities? Have you seen any of the protests? (or maybe taken part?) We've had race riots here too. But here it's between the Chinese and the Malays. A few years ago we had huge riots where 20 some people were killed and hundreds were injured. And then, Malaysia cut us off, so that Singapore became independent. People are worried now because England says it's going to pull all its military out by 1971 – what will happen then????

My parents are glad to be moving to England. We still don't know if we're coming through the US, so just keep HOPING! I'm crossing my fingers—so be ready!

> *Keep it Groovy.*
> *Henry*

P.S. My friend Tim was asking if your friend Anna could write to him. He saw the little note she wrote in one of your letters and said he would like to hear more from her. You can send me the letter and I will pass it on, but obviously, I need it soon as we'll be moving.

P.P.S. Hope you didn't eat too much cake at the wedding!

8 June 1968

On the morning of the wedding, sombre music poured out of the radio, replacing the usual mix of pop and country western songs. The DJs had only one topic to discuss –the funeral of Robert Kennedy in New York City.

Lizzie felt groggy from the night before. She wanted to roll over, turn her back to the sun pouring through the window and go back to sleep. The rehearsal dinner went on much longer than expected. Uncle Vinney and Aunt Gladys had come for the wedding from California. Vinney was Grandpa Ernest's brother who they only saw on special occasions. He always tried to capture the younger great nieces and give them a hug, drawing the heavy five o'clock shadow on his chin across their tender cheeks. Lizzie had reached an age where she tried to duck away from his embraces, especially when she had just tried some new makeup.

Where Grandpa Ernest was the stoic in the family, Uncle Vinney was the expressive one. He could embellish like no one else Lizzie knew and once he got started on a story, it was difficult to get away. It was a standing joke in the family that children had grown up and left home in the time it took Vinney to finish one of his tales. Her dad said Vinney should have been a used car salesman—the punters would have paid up just to get away. But despite that, they listened eagerly because the stories were always ridiculous and funny. Aunt Gladys just rolled her eyes, having heard it all time and time again.

"Lizzie, you'd better be up," Mom shouted up the stairs just as Lizzie was wrapping her dressing gown over her pajamas. The clink of plates could be heard from the kitchen.

Dad and her brothers were late coming in from the morning chores, having overslept after the late night. Breakfast was quickly dished out and they carried their plates into the living room to watch the funeral unfold live on TV.

"So many people – just look at those crowds." Her mother stared at the faces as the cameras panned the people on the street. Most were standing sombrely, others cried openly and a few had to be held up by police officers as they collapsed from grief and the warm day.

Lizzie and her brothers competed to spot the well-known faces as they arrived at the Cathedral entrance. Her mother's eyes hungrily followed Cary Grant as he walked into the building: he was one of her favourite actors. Musicians like Harry Belafonte mixed with politicians. The pending election was put to one side with Richard Nixon and President Johnson among the mourners. Johnny thought they should collect points for each one they saw, but their mother told him to be more respectful.

The Kennedy family arrived and Lizzie heard her mother stifle a gentle sob as she watched the pregnant widow surrounded by her 10 children. The service was a high Catholic mass in the huge St

Patrick's cathedral, heavy with ritual and pageantry. They sat transfixed by the strangeness of the ceremony -- a sharp contrast to their own simple Methodist services.

Suddenly, her mother jumped up shouting, "We're supposed to be there at 12!" She flicked off the TV and rushed everyone off to wash and dress. They had promised to meet at the church to help set up flowers and tables for the reception before the wedding at 2 pm.

After so many months of preparation and tedious discussions about flowers, cake, dresses and music, the wedding dissolved quickly into memories. There was the intake of breath when Grandpa Ernest walked Charlotte down the aisle with Grandma Mary beaming widely as her daughter was finally turned from tomboy into a triumph of lace. The new Uncle Joe stood expectantly by the altar ready for his bride.

This would be the last wedding for a while. It would be her generation next, Lizzie thought to herself, but she couldn't see Sam or Johnny getting married anytime soon. Sam had brought a couple of girls home, but no one that had lasted very long. Ellie had been nice – she used to talk to Lizzie about how to create the latest hairdos - but then that ended abruptly and Lizzie never heard what had happened.

There was a loud growl from Johnny's stomach just as the vows started. Lizzie glared at him to be quiet and he mimed back he couldn't help it – having had no lunch in the rush to get to the church.

Later, he would eat three pieces of cake in order to dampen the noise, but it was only when they returned home for the evening chores that he finally got a sandwich.

The reception was held in the utilitarian church hall where the Sunday school classes normally sat in circles on the metal chairs. The dull industrial beige of the walls had been enlivened with strips of pastel crepe paper strung into twisted swags and there were occasional baskets of flowers sitting on pillars.

The tiered cake decorated by a family friend with sugar roses and trailing leaves sat in the centre of a long linen-covered table. The new couple ceremoniously sliced into it and attempted to feed each other while photographs were taken for the album. Charlotte squashed the sticky chocolate sponge into Joe's mouth, splattering icing and crumbs across his face. He laughingly threatened to do the same to her but knew not to risk his new marital status by damaging her dress.

Dan always sniggered at the traditions, but Lizzie remembered he had done the same when he got married. Grandpa Ernest said it was good to see him in church but Dan replied it was only a flying visit. Lizzie thought she saw a little sadness on her grandfather's face but then he turned away to say something to Charlotte's new parents-in-law.

Jackie was wearing a new emerald green dress with an embroidered collar and seemed to be channelling the style of her namesake, Jackie

Kennedy. Even six months pregnant, she looked more chic than anyone else.

Lizzie sometimes tried to copy her style, but ended up being laughed at by Johnny instead who said she looked more carthorse than racing horse. It had taken three months of searching to find a dress for the wedding and still she had ended up with a simple A line dress that only just covered the worst of her shape. But the turquoise colour had lifted it out of the ordinary to make it feel special.

"It's a really good cake," Lizzie said to her aunt taking a forkful into her mouth.

"One of Dorothy's best, I'd say," Jackie replied. "Seems a shame to eat it so quickly."

Lizzie took this as a recommendation to eat more slowly, but Jackie appeared distracted as she looked over Lizzie's shoulder. Across the hall, Dan draped an arm over the back of a chair on which sat one of the bridesmaids, a friend of Charlotte's from college. His other arm was emphasizing the story Dan was telling the cluster of bridesmaids who made a polite titter at the punchline. Just then, Charlotte said she wanted to change into her 'going away' outfit, so the group quickly shrugged off Dan's attention and hurried to help her.

A small portable black and white television was brought in from the church office. It flickered images from the path of the train carrying Bobby Kennedy from New York to Washington. As it passed through small towns, hundreds lined the tracks standing in salute or waving a flag. White and black people mourned together. Soldiers stood to attention and families lined the rails waiting for a last glimpse.

4 June 2018

    Elizabeth dropped the heavy box she had brought home onto their dining table. She had avoided looking through her parents' collection of photos when they were at the farm house a few weeks before - the images of past lives had been still too painful to view, but now she felt drawn to those memories. She remembered seeing a small album from Charlotte's wedding. It was a homemade version of browning snapshots taken by her father. She found it two thirds of the way through the hundreds of photos.

    A slim radiant Charlotte beamed from the page. It had taken difficult and painful months to become this person. Elizabeth remembered the arguments at meals when her grandmother tried to get Charlotte to eat a bit more of the mashed potatoes and pork chop dinner. Charlotte resisted, knowing her stocky frame would be hard to mould into her dream dress, an empire waisted confection of trailing lace. She had dieted and planned and produced the perfect version of herself for the wedding.

    Grandma Mary had made so many comments about how lucky Charlotte had been to find someone to marry 'at her age' that Elizabeth grew up thinking of her as an old bride. But looking at the photo, she saw a fresh young face, so different to the aunt who had died six years ago. She searched the face in the photo for the features connecting the older, wedding image to her more recent memories. Charlotte had kept a sense of playfulness and banter. Her figure relaxed back into roundness with time but there had been more than a hint of the tomboy retained in her close cropped white hair.

A family photo slipped from the album as the glue came unstuck. It was the obligatory group shot of all the bride's family lined up on the church steps. Her grandparents stood on either side of the couple, looking confident and smug. The siblings and their children encircled the newlyweds.

Johnny and Sam competed with their tall father for space at the back but Elizabeth and her mother were pushed forward. Her aunt Barbara and husband Tom balanced them on the other side, restraining their 11 year old twin daughters who were always disappearing right when needed. Dan had his hand around Jackie's waist while grinning into the lens.

Her eyes slid across the faces and stopped on her own image. She had always hated seeing herself in photos. She didn't want to see what others saw – it was difficult enough being inside looking out. There had been so much angst about finding a dress - which became finding *any* dress - for the wedding. She had been too huge for anything special and in the end they thought this dress would just about do. Her mother told her it suited her, but Elizabeth remembered a feeling of disappointment. She stared at her younger self and was surprised to see that the colour set off her reddish hair. But even more surprising was that she looked 'normal'. She may not have been the prettiest, but she was far from grotesque. She wished she had known it then.

Richard pulled out one of the padded dining chairs and sat down. His hair was now flecked with grey, but with a steely shade that she found very attractive. He had become stockier over the last few years, but he gave her strength just as he did when they married 37 years ago.

"I wish Kiera's wedding would have been like this," he said picking up the album. "We would have saved a fortune!"

"Does seem simpler, doesn't it?" Elizabeth sighed. "No big, sit down dinner. No disco. No expensive venue."

"No booze?" Richard laughed. "Don't know if we would have survived it without the alcohol!"

"You say that now, but remember Jack? He could have done with a little *less* alcohol."

"Let it go," Richard countered, "There's always one in every family. He just happens to be in mine."

Richard took the group photo from her and peered through the faces. "Wow," he said, "look at you, all young and gorgeous!"

"If only," Elizabeth laughed.

"Is this your Uncle Dan, then?" Richard pointed at the photo. "You know, I've never seen a photo of him before? No one ever mentioned him either."

"This reminds me how much has been lost," Elizabeth said looking at her parents' smiling faces.

There had not been many from the photo left to come to her father's funeral. Charlotte died of bowel cancer. Barbara lived with her daughter Lisa in Arizona and Tom was in a nursing home. Elizabeth realised this was the last group photo of her father with all his family together – including Dan.

9 June 1968

The day after the wedding was Sunday and even though they had spent the previous day at the church, there was no excuse for missing the morning service according to Grandpa Ernest.

The five of them sat at the kitchen table after the milking and chores were done as her mother spooned up scrambled eggs with stacks of toast. Lizzie eyed the plates of food calculating their calories. She decided on two small scoops of egg and dug through the toast to find a dry half slice that had not been slathered in butter. She nibbled slowly so no one would comment on an empty plate. She still felt guilty about the cake she had eaten at the wedding. It was just tradition, she told herself, to have a piece of cake. But she could find no excuse for the second piece other than her own greed.

"I am so glad that's all over," said Johnny. "I couldn't take any more wedding talk. Finally we can do something else."

"Yeah," Sam said reaching past his brother for the jam. "Like you've got so much else to do. What've you got planned?"

"That depends..."

"What?" Sam laughed, "on whether you can borrow the car?"

"I could take the pick-up?" Johnny said hopefully.

Lizzie knew this discussion would go on all summer. As soon as her brothers got their driving licenses, the negotiations to use their sole car and the farm truck had begun.

The radio shifted from music to news: "Following the burial of Robert Kennedy yesterday, authorities have confirmed that the suspected killer of Martin Luther King, James Earl Ray, has been apprehended at an airport in London, England."

They looked at each other in surprise.

"At last," her father said. "Maybe the riots will stop now."

"It's not just about Martin Luther King, you know," Sam answered. "Everything King wanted is still waiting to happen."

Lizzie hoped the riots would stop as well, although they were only on the television. She had never met a Negro. There weren't any in Clarksburg. You'd have to go a city and they rarely left the county. The problem of segregation simply didn't come up in their day to day life. She had heard about the bus demonstration by Rosa Parks who refused to move to the 'coloured' part of the bus in

Montgomery, Alabama. It had happened when she was just a toddler and was part of the history of the civil rights movement they studied at school. She had never seen a coloured person, so she didn't know what discrimination was like, but then she had never seen a bus other than the big yellow one that took her to school.

It was another hot humid day when they arrived for the weekly service. Fans made from cardboard mounted on wooden sticks were handed out as they entered church. Lizzie wished she had worn a sleeveless blouse even if her thick upper arms would be on display. The synthetic fabric was clinging to the droplets running down her back. She whisked the fan back and forth trying to cool her reddening face.

The cavern of the church's sanctuary was divided by two aisles separating the three sections of long wooden pews. The rows were mostly full and they took seats toward the rear of the wide, central area. Grandpa Ernest and Grandma Mary sat erect in the second row from the front with Uncle Vinney and Aunt Gladys next to them. Lizzie picked out Anna across the room next to her parents and tried to catch her eye. Just when she thought Anna saw her, Johnny poked her with a hymnal. When she looked back, Anna had turned towards her mother.

The service always had the same format starting with hymns, prayers and a collection of weekly donations with bowls being passed down the rows of the congregation. By the time the sermon

started, Johnny was fidgeting, ready to be freed from his jacket and tie. Lizzie lost interest after the first ten minutes which the minister used to tell a short story for the children. Today it was the story of the good Samaritan, a story she had heard many times before. The toddlers sat at the back with their mothers, ready to be taken out if they began to cry. Lizzie sometimes wished she could join them.
The fan seemed to make the breeze hotter and when she leaned forward the back of the pew clawed at her blouse as it peeled off with a soft tearing sound. By the time for the final hymn, soft snores were heard from the row behind and Lizzie had to pinch herself to stop the heavy pull on her own eyelids.

    A light breeze welcomed them as they poured outside onto the church steps. Lizzie rushed up behind Anna who was leaning against the iron railing.

    "Finally. I've been wanting to see you," She said before stopping as Anna turned towards her.

    Her friend was pale, especially in the brightness of the summer sun.

    "I thought she should come to church," Anna's mother put in, "even though she told me she didn't feel up to it. I thought it was just too many late nights, but you can see she's not well."

    "I can speak for myself," Anna grumped.

    "I'm so sorry," Lizzie tried to contain her disappointment. "I've been wanting to talk to you all week. You know, about Henry?"

    Anna seemed disorientated.

    "You know, my pen pal?"

Anna nodded slightly.

"Not here, though," Lizzie said giving a quick look over her shoulder to see if any of her family were nearby.

Anna covered her mouth protectively.

"Maybe later in the week, huh? When she's feeling better?" Anna's mother led her away.

Lizzie nodded in agreement hoping whatever her friend had wasn't contagious. She didn't want to come down with something at the beginning of the summer holiday. On the other hand, a virus could stop her eating as much. What a way to lose weight, she thought as they headed to the car.

Grandpa Ernest and Uncle Vinney were talking to her father. The three heads seemed to have been shaped in the same mould. Grandpa and her dad's ruddy complexion stopped two thirds of the way up their foreheads at the point where a baseball cap normally sat as they worked in the sun. Wisps of hair had been brushed across Grandpa Ernest's smooth head. When her father leaned forward, Lizzie could see his hair was beginning to thin as well and the faint outline of a bald centre was beginning to show.

She glanced at her brothers across the street and smirked – their impossibly full heads of hair were at risk if genetics took their toll. They weren't allowed to let it grow long like the photos of rock bands she saw in magazines.   Sam's sideburns had extended down his jawline while he was away at college, she noticed, but he wasn't ready to challenge his father to let the auburn locks grow below the collar line.

In the photo, Henry's hair was already down to his shoulders. That was longer than was allowed in her family. She wondered how long Henry wanted to grow it. What would her family think if they DID come to visit? Could her father keep from saying something? Grandpa Ernest would look very stern but not mention it. Grandma Mary would definitely have some comments and probably not very positive or polite ones.

Her father always had the 'short back and sides' treatment - nearly a military scalping when it was freshly done. He said it was only hippies, who needed a good bath, that wore their hair long.

Hair had become a political statement for the young. There was even a new musical out called 'Hair', although that was as much a protest against the War as it was about hair. Her mother was scandalised by the reviews of the show which said there was nudity on stage. Hair, nakedness, drugs and the War had all become so tightly enmeshed, that one couldn't be separated from the others. The subject even came up as the family gathered around Grandma Mary's extended table for Sunday lunch.

"You must get lots of them hippies in California," her father said to Uncle Vinney. "Don't know how you put up with 'em."

"Most of them are students. They stay on campus a lot."

"Can't stand the hair." Her father forked out a piece of chicken onto his plate from the dish that was being passed around the table. "You can tell the ones on drugs by looking at the hair." He eyed the edges of Sam's hair scraping the top of his collar.

"There've been so many coming through on their way to San Francisco," Aunt Gladys said. "Fortunately they don't stay near us but there are often van loads of them getting gas and eating at the diners on their way through."

"Leave a pile of rubbish," Uncle Vinney added.

"Oh, not always. And, you wouldn't have got your tire changed if that VW hadn't stopped to help."

"They just look so ridiculous," Grandpa Ernest put in. "Never would have been allowed when I was young." Without looking, Lizzie knew her father felt he had been accused of being responsible for any fault that lay with the younger generation.

"Nothing was allowed when you were young, Dad," Dan smirked. "You were all sent out to work at 10 and never had any fun, I'm sure."

"It wasn't that bad," Vinney said. "The dances were always good. That's how your Dad courted your Mom, you know."

"Yeah, I've heard the story—in Fenton, in the town hall," Dan replied. "Think that was the last time he went dancing. I've never seen him out – not even a square dance!"

"Hard work running a farm and raising a family," Grandpa Ernest humphed.

Just then Simon swung his arms out to his father to be released from the high chair. With a hefty tug Dan pulled the two year old from the seat and sat him on his lap. Simon grabbed a pea from his father's plate and squished it onto the tablecloth. Grandma Mary smiled but Lizzie could see she was inwardly calculating how to remove the stain.

"Wait until you have another one," his father went on. "There's always something to keep an eye on. Kids are always finding things to get into. Even when they're grown up."

"Yeah, and two at a time is even harder," Barbara told her brother while the twins pulled faces in protest.

"Well, I think we'll stop at two, thank you very much," Dan said. "Really don't want any more. Would be great to have a little girl, though." Jackie was smiling. "Perfect."

The plates were passed to Grandma Mary who scraped off any remains and stacked them. Lizzie had tried to eat as little as possible, but at the same time did not want to be noticed for wasting food. It was a fine balance between an acceptable portion size and the amount that could be left. But the scales tipped towards eating when Lizzie saw Grandma Mary carry in her favourite pie, homemade lemon meringue with a sharp base piled high with the sweet fluffy cloud. One more day off the diet couldn't really make that much difference she told herself.

9 June 2018

Elizabeth decided mornings were the best time of day. She had taken early retirement the year before, just when her father became ill. It had given her time to be with him but meant that she was only just now working out how to cope with her new spare time. Richard chided her that someone had to pay the bills which is why he kept on working, but she knew he still enjoyed the challenge of the ever changing IT market. He had gone off this morning humming lightly under his breath as she put the coffee maker on for another cup.

She sat in the breakfast nook with a view over their backyard. The sun was filtering through the leafy trees. A sparrow hopped across a branch to the feeder she had put up near the window. Pigeons and sparrows were her most frequent diners, but occasionally the brightly coloured goldfinches or red cardinals pecked at the seeds.

The smell of roasted coffee beans spread across the room. A light snapped on indicating another brew was ready. The sparrow startled when she rose from the chair and threatened to fly away but settled back to eat as she poured a cup of coffee.

She had known as soon as they first walked through the door that this was their forever home. That had been 29 years ago when they needed to replace their compact townhouse with something larger. It had taken a lot of inspiration to look past the dated décor and the overgrown garden to see the possibilities but it had grown into their vision.

Stripping back the walls to their bare bones and re-covering them to their own taste had taken years. They cleared out the chimney and rebuilt the fireplace for cosy winter nights. The breakfast corner was added when they extended the kitchen but now she couldn't remember it not being there.

Kiera loved the garden. The previous elderly owners had not been able to manage its upkeep and let it subside into long grass and weeds. Richard and Elizabeth had hacked it back while Kiera picked buttercups from the lawn. They dug out the flower beds and planted perennials which came back every year. In the humid hot days of summer, they erected a temporary swimming pool in which Kiera splashed for hours at a time. She had Richard's tanning gene and turned a golden brown while Elizabeth crisped into an increasingly brighter pink in the sun.

There was a single donut left in the fridge from the pack of Dunkin' Donuts' best which they had consumed over the weekend. Elizabeth slid it onto a plate and placed it next to the steaming coffee cup. She licked off the cream escaping from the donut's centre before taking her first bite. She knew bran flakes would have been a better choice for breakfast but the lure of a sweet treat to savour in solitude seemed too luxurious to ignore.

She stared at the box with the embroidered lid. It had time travelled her back to another world and a different version of herself, mixing with the memories of her family and childhood. Richard had not asked about it. But then, she told herself, she hadn't looked through it while he was around. Despite all the years passing, the letters felt too personal to share.

She wiped her sticky fingers across a napkin and pushed back the lid. Past several blue aerogram letters there was a thicker envelope. The edges had worn from use but inside she could see a string of little hearts and she knew immediately when it had arrived.

14 February 1968

There was a poster on the notice board for the Valentine's dance on Friday. Lizzie hated Valentine's Day. The dance this year meant the love fest was extended by two days with all its added torture. She scoffed at the couples crowded into the corners of the cafeteria that lunch time while inwardly jealous. It was a day of red hearts, chocolates and corny messages of love and she wanted to be part of it.

The previous year she had desperately wanted to be noticed by Daniel, who sat opposite her during English literature. But Lizzie had seen him with Jane from the debate club at the basketball game the weekend before Valentine's and on the most romantic day of the year, they were walking down the hallway, hands entwined and heads close together. She had vowed not to care about it this year, but she couldn't help it.

Anna would get Valentine cards. She always did. Lizzie's friend was a magnet for teenage boys, whether she wanted their attention or not. Lizzie thought it was the long blonde hair that slipped halfway down her back. It shimmered in the sunlight, something Lizzie had never been able to achieve despite using conditioner and lengthy brushing. Anna could flick her hair with the bounce of a shampoo ad.

Lizzie spied her friend at a table across the room with her mac and cheese lunch on the tray in front of her. Wayne Johnson sat next to her leaning in close to speak in her ear while Anna tilted in a diplomatic angle away from him. Lizzie dropped her tray loudly, startling Wayne away from his prey. Anna smiled thankfully at her.

"Happy V Day," Lizzie said. "Going to the dance?"

"Joe asked," Anna replied, "but I was hoping Gary would."

Wayne looked momentarily upset. "You could go with me," he suggested.

"Not going to happen. But maybe you could take Lizzie?"

Lizzie scowled.

"Nah," Wayne countered, "I don't take second best."

"Oh, you'll be lucky to take anyone then," Anna laughed.

Lizzie turned her head so they wouldn't notice the hurt on her face. Her friend hadn't even noticed the sting in her suggestion. Wayne lumbered out of the chair in defeat and left the girls alone.

"Didn't know you were keen on Gary. Thought he was dating Susan."

Anna broke into a large smile. "I heard they had a huge fight and that it's over. So, I can hope!"

At that moment the door to the cafeteria swung open and Gary walked in with an arm around Susan's waist. They smiled at each other and headed for the food counter.

"Well, so much for that then," Lizzie said with only a hint of smugness.

"Guess there's always Joe. What about you? Who're you going with?"

Lizzie laughed a little too sharply. "Don't think dances are my scene."

"Come on," Anna urged. "I let you off last time for that lame excuse, but you really need to TRY to come to some of the dances. How're you going to catch a guy otherwise?"

"Haven't you heard? There's women's lib – we don't have to have a man anymore to have a life." Lizzie felt angry her friend kept pushing the point. She didn't want to admit she knew no one would want to dance with her. She learned that lesson in junior high and it was embarrassing to sit by the wall all evening. For two hours she waited in the melee of hormones and possibilities, tapping her foot in rhythm with the music and holding a slight smile of interest on her face. Anna had disappeared into the middle of the hopping mass, returning only briefly to cool down before being pulled back to the dancing. The corners of Lizzie's mouth had begun to ache and the smile sharpened into despair.

Afterwards, Anna accused her of not trying to join in. It was the biggest fight they ever had. Lizzie wanted to tell her how much she hated sitting on the side, but that getting up was even harder for her. For Anna, there was no conflict – if she wanted to dance, she just got up and did it. She had no sympathy for those who didn't have a go. Lizzie envied her, but knew she couldn't do the same. She was embarrassed to admit how hurt she felt sitting on the side that night. While invisible when her classmates selected dance partners, she felt she was a target for ridicule as a wallflower.

It was a night she never wanted to repeat but Anna wouldn't let it go.

"Well, I didn't know you were turning into a lesbian!! I didn't think we had any of those in Indiana! Or at least in our school," Anna smirked.

Lizzie gritted her teeth, unsure how to react. It was a word she didn't know but understood admitting that could have more consequences.

"Tell you what," Anna went on, "I'll ask you to dance. But would that make me a lesbian as well?"

"Who's a lesbian?" Gary paused by their table. "That you, Anna?"

Anna flushed with embarrassment, but quickly replied, "How could you ever think that? No, it's Lizzie who's thinking about joining that club."

"I only said I didn't want to go to the dance," Lizzie muttered. "Nothing else."

"Just as well, then," Gary laughed. "Don't think there'll be too many lezzies to dance with." He turned back to Anna. "Unless, you were joining her?" His left eyebrow was raised quizzically but Lizzie suspected arrogance in his smile.

"I'm willing to prove that I'm not." Anna flicked the shimmering hair and gave him her most sultry smile.

"I might take you up on that," Gary said just before Susan came up behind him and tugged him away from the table.

Anna turned back to Lizzie. "Well, that's done it then. I thought you could dance with me, but Gary'll get the wrong idea now." Without waiting for a reply, Anna got up and carried her tray back to a collection point and left the cafeteria leaving Lizzie alone at the table.

The next morning, Anna brushed a light dusting of snow from her coat as she boarded the school bus. She smiled at Lizzie without any mention of the embarrassment from the day before. Lizzie knew for them to remain friends, she must bite back any bitterness.

"Still going to the dance with Joe?" she asked Anna.

"Haven't had a better offer – so I guess so," her friend answered. "Gary looks like he'll be busy. Maybe I can convince him to give me one dance at least."

"He's a player."

"I know," Anna conceded, "but if he's on your arm, you can get on the A table. That's all I'm really aiming at.

"I've heard he's a bit of an octopus when you're on your own."

"Just watch me handle it," Anna threw over her shoulder as they separated for their classes.

The thick envelope was waiting for her later in a pile of mail that had been abandoned on her father's desk until he came in from the fields. As she opened the card, a smile erupted across her mouth in disbelief.

8 February 1968

Allo ma cherie.

I am hoping this reaches you in time. What will you be doing for Valentine's Day? My band is playing for a dance at my school. I think it's just 'cause they can get us cheap! We're pretty good at Beatles songs. James, our drummer, is more a Rolling Stones fan, but we have to be careful about what we play – the teachers don't like the songs to get too RUDE! Some people at church actually think that Mick Jagger made a deal with the devil and that's why they have done so well. We've got a couple of teachers who think like that as well so they don't want us to play the Stones at all. CENSORSHIP! We feel verrrrry oppressed. What do you think?

We're lucky to be allowed to play at the dance. A lot of guys in my class have to put in extra time at the end of the day in detention. Last week when we were changing after our P E class, a bunch of the guys got together and grabbed my mate Paul when he was mid-changing. They stripped off his shorts so he was completely naked and shoved him into the girls' changing room and held the door shut. The girls had been taking their showers, so they didn't have clothes on either. Man, there was a lot of screaming (and banging on the door by Paul)!!!

The PE teacher came running very quickly. He started shouting as well – mostly to open up the door so Paul could get out. The girls screamed some more when they thought a MALE teacher was coming into their room!

It ended up that everyone who was there, even the innocent bystanders (ME included), got hauled up in front of the headteacher. Fortunately, I only got two days in detention but others got two weeks. Paul was so embarrassed after this, he couldn't look at any of the girls without going all red. But he became very popular with the guys in the class when he told them what he had seen!

Have you got snow? It's still hot – like 85 to 90°F EVERY day. It would be great to have a change with some very cool weather. Plus, I've never made a snowball or a snowman and I would really like to do that!! If you make one, can you send me photos? Maybe it will make me feel cooler just looking at it.

note on the fridge to put milk or coffee or bacon on the shopping list. Although she recognised the shape of his writing, she had never found deciphering the scratchings easy. For the most part, she found it uninteresting or unintelligible as it related to some IT problem Richard was working on at the time. Computer jargon was another foreign language she had not learned.

Most of his written communication to her was now contained in the abused language of texting – brief and stripped of sentiment. There was occasionally an 'X' at the end of the message and from that she accepted the love they assumed of each other. It was natural, she told herself, after 37 years of marriage not to have to prove your love in soppy demonstrations. They were settled with each other. The exception was their wedding anniversary when Richard would always pick out an embossed card with the longest essay from the Card Boutique. It was never one of the cheap thin ones from the card outlet store. And every year, there was a single red rose. It was just his way of reminding her that he did still love her.

There hadn't been many Valentine cards over the years. Richard didn't see the point of the day. He eventually learned to deliver a card but it always felt purchased out of duty and never had the same power of that first Valentine from Henry.

She met Richard through Gloria and Bill who were holding a 4th of July barbecue in 1980. Most of her friends were married after finding their partners at college. Some had even started parenthood which made her single status even more extraordinary. She had felt awkward at these gatherings. Bridget Jones had been right to call them smug marrieds, she thought. The phrase hadn't been invented then yet though, so she just tried to pass off questions about her love life as immaterial.

Richard had been invited to the barbecue to balance the threat of a single woman. He worked with Bill providing technical support to offices. Big companies still maintained payroll and other records on computer punch cards. Bill and Richard battled system failures and upgrades. It was an early love of Richard's that Elizabeth never felt she quite surpassed.

The bonding over charred meat led to other dates and their wedding the following year. Her friends were glad to be released from headhunting. Elizabeth could hear the relief in her mother's voice when she rang to let her parents know about the engagement. Just like her grandmother, her mother had feared her daughter was becoming too old for marriage.

It was a simple wedding held at the same Methodist Church she attended when she was young. Just like her Aunt Charlotte, she was walked proudly down the aisle by her father, while Sam and JJ sat with their own families. Sam had two boys by then and JJ's daughter was 2 and he had a second baby on the way.

Aunt Barbara and Uncle Tom were there with one of the twins. Lisa had moved out to California but Laura had come back to Clarksburg after going to college. Jackie had sent a card for her, Dan, Simon and Sandy who was then 13.

Her life since had been chronicled in the row of photos across the top of the sideboard: she and Richard smiling deeply into each other's eyes while standing in front of the church after the wedding ceremony, photos of the baby Kiera in their first home, and snapshots from vacations taken at the seaside or 'out west'. The younger images of their parents were a cruel reminder of time passing and opportunities missed. She had wanted to have her parents record their family stories as an oral history to keep for the generations to follow. It's too late, she thought as she looked at the photo of her mother laughing as she gathered in her children in their Sunday best clothes. There were so many questions she could have asked, but now she would never be able to hear their answers. The regret pressed down heavily on her.

Asking questions was harder than she had thought. She didn't know how to pick open the secrets that had haunted the family since she was young. She had delayed so she could find the right way to phrase her questions, but time had passed and now her parents were no longer able to give any answers.

Looking at the box of letters, she realised that Henry was another mystery in her life. Of all the people who could have replied to her small ad in the church's international newsletter asking for a pen friend, Henry was the surprising result. Elizabeth closed up the box and stroked the soft lid gently. He had given her a different outlook to the world but what had she given him?

When they were teenagers, she wondered why he was interested in writing to her. Life on the plains of Indiana was a routine of chores and events that rotated but never changed. The year was divided into the seasons and the jobs that had to be done in each one to keep the farm productive. From spring through to autumn, there were fields that had to be worked and even winter was controlled by the twice daily cycle of milking. There were meetings that were attended monthly and churches attended weekly. Everything was scheduled and expected – there were few surprises.

Elizabeth realised now that what had been so ordinary for her was exotic to someone living in a city, removed from a life connected to the cycles of the earth, plants and animals. He wouldn't have known that the smell of spring was not the scent of rain, but the stench of barns being cleared and the manure spread across the fields. Summer was not made of lazy days sipping drinks in the shade, but a frenzy to harvest and store food for both humans and animals for the winter.

She looked out to the backyard. There were no long fields of corn, just the edges of three neighbouring houses with yards that squared up to theirs. She was now a city girl but, like every former farmer, she had a few rows of vegetables in a sunny spot – just a reminder of another time and a connection to the past.

The box was another link to a time that couldn't be forgotten. He was so absolutely gorgeous. Elizabeth smiled to herself thinking of his long hair framing the dark eyes. The longing she felt from the letters swallowed her when they met. She expected to be tongue tied but they had talked and talked and it felt so easy. She could no longer remember what they said, but the surprise of how good their time together was remained with her.

There was a flutter deep in her stomach which she hoped was hunger, but suspected wasn't. She gathered up the box and put it on a shelf in the sideboard, under some magazines she was saving for later. There was time to go through the recipe cards and find something special for their supper. Richard deserved that. He worked so hard. He was her rock. She would make sure to find something he would like.

18 June 1968

It was more than a week after the wedding before Lizzie had a chance to see Anna. Henry's letter had been burning through her self-confidence as the days passed. She managed to cut down the portions on her plate without anyone commenting although her mother paused and watched her when Lizzie passed the cookie plate without taking one to accompany her fruit salad. She volunteered to walk the drinks for the workers out to the fields and tried running circles around the barn when no one was around. The bathroom scales told her that morning that she had lost two pounds since the arrival of Henry's first threat.

Anna said she would be home that morning and Lizzie was anxious to finally see her. They still hadn't made any plans for the summer vacation. Usually, they met up at least once a week to ride their bikes out for a picnic, spend the day baking a mountain of cakes or splash around in Anna's swimming pool once it had been pulled from storage and erected.

The road into town was bumpy but there were few vehicles. She fought to pass a tractor pulling a flat trailer but in the end she let it lead until Mr. Cutler drove it into a field entrance on his farm and waved as she rode past.

The heatwave from the wedding weekend had eased and the cooler morning was perfect for the ride. Lizzie hammered the pedals for an extra workout and the bike shot along, spraying stones and startling birds pecking at the remains of animals who were victims of the road.

Anna was waiting for her on their front porch, swinging gently on the bench hung from a rafter with chains. A library book lay next to her, upside down on the page where she stopped reading. The golden hair was pulled back tightly into a ponytail, making her face sharper.

"Wow. You look like you've gone 3 rounds with Muhammed Ali!"

"Thanks," Lizzie replied with sarcasm. "I was just trying to work off as many calories as I could."

"That red face should cook some off! Is it working?"

Lizzie beamed. "Two pounds already! Given the wedding was in the middle of my dieting time, I think that's pretty good. Can you see a difference?"

Anna shook her head regretfully.

"Wish now I hadn't eaten so much last weekend, but it's too late."

"So I can't get you a soda?"

"Only if it's doesn't have calories."

Anna ducked through the front door and re-emerged carrying a glass bottle of sugar free TAB and another of orange pop. They pulled off the caps and let the cold drinks fizz down their throats.

"You survived the wedding then?"

"Yeah, I'm glad it's over now though. There were too many relatives visiting and it all meant eating so many meals together."

"Thought you would have liked that!" Anna scoffed.

"You know I like the food," Lizzie sighed. "That's the problem. I have got to lose a lot of this excess fat – fast!" She slapped a wobbly thigh.

"The reason being….?"

"I told you, didn't I?" Lizzie had a moment's confusion. "Henry may be coming to visit!!"

"Henry?"

"You know-- my pen pal in Singapore. By the way, a friend of his saw what you wrote in my letter to him and says he wants to write to YOU. Should I give him your address so he can write?"

Now Anna seemed confused. "Sure, I suppose he can. But Henry is coming here?"

"They're moving to England and might come through the US on their way. He wants to come and see me! I haven't even sent him a proper photo yet. How can I meet him like this?" Lizzie waved her arms over the length of her body. Despair washed over her. She had held this secret close, afraid to make it real. Telling someone about it created a tidal wave of anxiety she felt unable to control.

Anna was silent as she surveyed Lizzie, taking in the uncooperative fly-away hair, the stained T shirt and the rounded stomach. Lizzie felt the tug of her gaze trying to mould her into something better. A pent-up breath escaped when Anna turned to pick up her drink.

"He really digs you," Anna said finally, "or he wouldn't keep writing. And he hasn't seen your picture, so it must not matter to him!"

It wasn't the absolution Lizzie craved.

"What would you do if he does come? I mean, with your family, his family….?"

"I don't know." Lizzie was afraid to admit she had not even thought about those problems, having been so focussed on worrying about what Henry would think of her. But how would her family react, she suddenly wondered. Sam and Johnny were sure to make jokes about her and poke fun at Henry if they could. She cringed thinking what her father might say with his views on foreigners. Her mother would just put more place settings on the table and welcome them. But what , she suddenly thought, would his family think of them? They were, after all, just a simple farming family. They hadn't even been outside the country.

A dark green pick-up truck turned onto the street, a cloud of gray fumes puffing from its exhaust. They watched it slow as the driver read the name on the mail box and then moved on to the next house where it paused again. At the third house, the truck stopped and the driver got out. The banging on the door carried across the still morning and they heard a babbled exchange between the driver and someone in the house. The driver returned to his truck and it chugged on its way spewing more fumes into the air.

"Sorry about being so busy with all this family stuff," Lizzie said finally, deciding a change of topic was best. "What've you been doing – how was the hayride? I meant to warn you about Eric Hayden. I overheard him bragging about what he'd like to do with you. Sorry."

"Eric?" Anna looked surprised. "I'd rather not talk about it," she said after a long pause. "It was embarrassing. They were mostly all juniors and seniors and they made me feel like a little baby in the group. But I showed them I wasn't."

They sipped their drinks in silence. Lizzie watched battling emotions cross her friend's face. It was always easy to tell when Anna was worried or sad. Today, she looked both.

"What'd you do?"

"Doesn't matter now," Anna evaded. "I just wish I hadn't gone that night."

Lizzie started to ask what had happened, but she could feel a distance swelling between them that she didn't know how to cross. Anna was swaying slowly on the swing bench watching as the neighbour's mottled tabby stretched out in a warming circle of sunlight. One of her kittens from the spring litter wobbled around a flower pot and pounced on her from behind before settling into the curvature of his mother for a tongue wash.

"Did you watch all the funeral on TV?" Lizzie said to break the quiet. "We had a television at the wedding reception so that people could watch it. It felt weird looking at a funeral while we were eating wedding cake."

Anna turned toward her. "Yeah, really sad. It must've been hard on your aunt Charlotte and all the family."

"I don't think anything could've stopped her and Joe enjoying the day. The grown-ups were pretty upset about it, but my cousins, the twins, didn't seem to care at all. I remember crying when JFK was killed and I was younger than them. Jackie was the most upset. She seemed grumpy, but then she's so pregnant. It must be hard carrying all that around with you. Mind you, I reckon I'm probably carrying that much extra. Gotta lose this fast...."

"Have you told your mom and dad about Henry coming?" Anna, as usual, hit upon Lizzie's Achilles heel.

"They've been so busy...." Lizzie qualified without conviction.

"What! So these foreigners show up suddenly one day – you don't think they'll notice?"

The image of such a meeting with her father coming fresh from the milking parlour, smelling of sour manure flashed into her head. Her mother in her ragged garden shirt and dirt still under her fingernails would welcome them in.

"Okay, okay. I'll tell them," Lizzie finally agreed. "But it's a least another month before anyone could turn up. Their school gets out a lot later than ours. So there's no rush."

21 June 2018

Elizabeth scrubbed around the sink in the guest en suite. Kiera was bringing Zoe to stay for a few days as Dave had a business trip that wouldn't wait. He had promised to cut down on time away from home to spend more time with their newborn, but said that this one couldn't be avoided. They were still getting used to being parents and coping with the broken sleep. It was Dave's suggestion that Kiera come stay with them but Elizabeth could hear the relief in her daughter's voice when she asked if it would be all right.

As much as she wanted to see her granddaughter, Elizabeth also welcomed the distraction from the temptation to sit and read through Henry's old letters. She felt haunted by the ghost of feelings from another era. She had always believed the past was gone and needed to stay there, but the letters were a physical conduit to someone she used to be.

The television was playing in the background for company as she cleaned. Elizabeth had given up watching the news. The cycle was now so quick that any statement President Trump made was cancelled out by his next. She couldn't believe that the country had elected this man into office, She recalled a trip back to Indiana when the candidates were still posturing before the primaries. Trump had been the least likely candidate and her family discounted his chances of winning. But they left a caveat that if he did win through the primaries, well, anyone was better than Hilary. It was a moment that worried her when all the pundits were certain that Hilary Clinton would win over the bumbling Donald Trump.

His current row was over the migrant children held along the Mexican border. They were being held separately from their parents, including toddlers and babies. The reports coming out showed pictures of the children in what looked like cages. One story told how older children had to care for a baby who was separated from his aunt. Elizabeth shuddered to think of Zoe being taken away in such circumstances. The thought of her granddaughter sent a wave a desire through her to hold the tiny girl close.

A photo of Senator John McCain and his daughter flashed on the TV screen. Elizabeth turned the sound up slightly to catch Meghan say that President Trump's comments about her father at a rally the previous evening in Duluth were gross. The President was blaming the Senator for the failure to repeal the Affordable Care Act –

the healthcare package known as Obamacare. The year before, the Senator had travelled back to Washington from Arizona especially for the vote, having only just received a diagnosis of brain cancer.

The reporter said someone had shouted out that McCain had been a war hero, but the President ignored it. Elizabeth remembered the disbelief people felt when Trump said before the election that McCain was not a war hero. The senator was captured while fighting in Vietnam and held captive for more than five years. During the election campaign, Trump famously said that his rival was a not a hero because he was captured and he didn't like people who were captured. Trump avoided the draft and never served in Vietnam. He used the college deferments which Elizabeth's brothers had hoped on to avoid being drafted.

When Sam came home after his first year at college, the rules changed. The war was using up young men. Unlike their father's generation, this was a war of division both in Vietnam and at home. Protesters campaigned across the country against US involvement in the war. Thousands fled north over the Canadian border to avoid being taken into the military – and young men collected their mail with trepidation.

18 June 1968

Lizzie stopped her bike by the mailbox at the end of their lane. She scanned through the envelopes to make sure there weren't any foreign letters among them. The local newspaper was rolled up inside its own box and she pulled it out and wrapped it around the letters.

Her mother was pulling weeds in the flower bed at the corner of the house. There were just a few areas of vibrant colour in the expanse of green lawn. Flowers for cutting were planted beside the vegetable garden, but the plantings next to the house were her mother's pride. She pushed back the auburn hair from her glistening forehead. Lizzie notice a few strands of white were showing among the darker hair.

"Thought you'd be longer with Anna," she said, gathering up the pile of weeds.

"She's got to go into Fenton this afternoon." Lizzie followed as her mother dropped the weeds on to a compost heap and headed into the house.

"You'll have time now to mow the lawn then," her mother said over her shoulder. Lizzie glanced at the lush green where she would spend the afternoon running up and down on the ride-on mower. She grinned at the prospect as she loved to drive the miniature tractor.

Sam and Johnny usually drove the big tractors while working, but a couple of times they had let her have a go. She was still trying to master letting the clutch out gently. It was a huge lever on the side of the engine and when she followed Sam's instruction to let it out, it crashed into gear making the tractor jump forward and sending Sam flying off the hitch onto the ground. It was a bit of slapstick that Sam had not appreciated. The lawn mower was much simpler to operate and it gave her a chance to drive before she was old enough to go on the roads.

Her mother held the screen door open for Lizzie and then laid down the hoe and trowel on the porch floor. She picked up two wooden punnets and handed them to Lizzie.

"Pick some strawberries and we'll have shortcake for lunch," her mother said disappearing into the coolness of the house.

Gathering a small amount of berries didn't take long. Lizzie could see that the bulk of the crop was just about ready. That would mean afternoons of making jam and freezing berries to put on ice cream or in fruit salad during the winter months. Years before, her mother had planted four long rows of strawberries. It was the one continuous patch of the garden and every year they re-fruited with more abundance than they could use. Her mother frantically gave baskets out to family and friends after they had stored enough for themselves.

Lizzie stood looking out the kitchen window as she washed and hulled the berries. She caught the first scent of the shortcake rising in the oven and her tummy gave a little growl. There was nothing like fresh strawberry shortcake. The fruit must be good for her, she debated to herself, trying to avoid the fact she would eat the dessert regardless.

She heard a sudden hiss from her mother who had been looking through the bundle of letters Lizzie had carried into the house. She turned and saw it was not the letters but the newspaper that caught her mother's attention. On the lower half of the front page, below a story about the latest battle between President Johnson and Congress, was a photo of a young man in uniform. Fred O'Neill had been in Sam's class from grade school through to high school graduation. The two boys had been put together as playmates when they were young as the parents sat at nearby picnic tables and watched, but over time they had evolved their own set of friends. After they received their diplomas the previous summer, Sam left for college and Fred enlisted in the army.

"I can't believe it." Lizzie could hear the tears in her mother's voice. "Ruth must be devastated. I can't imagine how you cope...."

Lizzie put an arm around her mother's suddenly shaking shoulders. A splash of teardrop fell on the newspaper page, blurring the line that read 'Local boy missing in action.' They stood in awkward silence for just a moment before her mother took a deep breath and pulled back her shoulders.

"I'll make another shortcake to take over to them," she said pulling her upper arm across her cheeks.

The men came in from the fields smelling of sweet new hay just as her mother was pulling a meatloaf out of the oven. The shortcake was cooling on a wire rack. There were potatoes baked in butter and their own milk with the first of the green beans from the garden and some sweetcorn from the freezer.

Johnny started slathering a piece of bread with butter before he was told with a look to bow his head to say grace. Lizzie lifted her head as it ended just in time to catch the gentle squeeze of her mother's hand on top of her father's square rough hand and she knew that her father had seen the paper on his way to sit down. They ate without talking, allowing a war thousands of miles away to dominate the conversation.

Sam finally spoke as the plates were scraped and cleared away. "It may be nothing," he said. "Could just have gotten separated and he'll catch up soon. Doesn't say what they're doing to find him."

"Nothing we can do here but wait – and pray," her father replied.

Lizzie knew he wasn't just thinking about Fred, but if her brothers were called up, it could be them who were lost. Johnny wouldn't turn 18 until the end of the summer. He was one of the youngest in his class which for once was a good thing as it meant he still had months before he was even eligible to be drafted. Sam got a deferment for his first year at college, but the rules were changed and another deferment was not guaranteed. A notice to go to the draft board could come any day.

The meal suddenly lay heavily on her stomach and Lizzie eyed the shortcake covered in strawberries and cream with disinterest. The others picked at the edges of the dessert except for Johnny who spooned it hastily into his mouth and looked for more.

"I'll take a shortcake over later to the O'Neills," her mother said. "I don't know what else we can do."

When the men had returned to the fields, Lizzie went to the garage, unscrewed the cap on the gas tank of the mower and poured in more fuel. She pushed it out of the door and then threw her leg over the seat and settled in. It started with the first turn of the key and she rattled along the drive to the edge of the yard before making the first circuit. On the return to her starting point, she saw the trail of dust that flew up as her mother drove out the lane with the shortcake and a punnet of strawberries lying on the passenger seat.

21 August 1969

Ma Cherie, Lizzie,

How is your vacation going? It's so different here in England to what we had in Singapore. I can't believe how cold the summers are by comparison. They say we've had a 'good' summer but that means it's only about 72 F. We'd be putting on jumpers (sweaters to you) if it was that temperature in Singapore!!

But today's at least dry and I've been sitting in our back garden under a tree reading your last letter to me. I was going to write sooner, but had to recover from the shock of what your friends wrote in it. Man, you are CORRUPTING me. I've got to work harder to keep my reputation! See what you've driven me to?......

I've missed my old friends from Singapore over the past year. A couple of them have written, but not much. Tim told me he had a couple of letters from your friend Anna, but then he didn't hear any more. He said she was slowly getting used to her new school. She was upset because her family had to move away. Sounded like it was going to be hard for her dad to find another job. Do you write to her? I don't hear much from the guys back in Singapore. I suppose we'll just drift apart eventually. Do you think that will happen to US?

It will be time to head back to school and the books soon. I've got 'O' levels this year. I need good grades so I can move up to college (kind of like your high school). I want to go to university, but will need top marks to do it. We're lucky in England to get free tuition – what about you? Do you think you will go to university? I think I'd like to be a lawyer, but that takes extra years to train.

I hope you aren't TOO offended by the headline news I have included – do you have news like this? It's just so PERVERTED!!

Write soon, if you can.
Love, Henry.

21 June 2018

"Geez, Mom," Kiera shouted out. "What's all this?"

Elizabeth hadn't heard the door. Her daughter was standing in the centre of the kitchen staring at one of

Henry's letters spread across the table. Elizabeth had forgotten to gather in the collage of ancient headlines shaped into a letter. 'TEACHER IN TRYST' and 'LOVERS LOST OVER EDGE' screamed out in bold type. She tried not to look at the photo of a man working on a chastity belt over the headline 'Brit finds new market'.

"They're just some old letters."

"Don't think they're from Dad," Kiera said. "Not really his style."

"No, just from a pen pal I had a long time ago," Elizabeth admitted. "I found them at your grandpa's house when we were clearing out."

"What, you've kept them all this time?"

"They just got left behind," Elizabeth shrugged. "That's all."

"Look pretty racy. Didn't know you had it in you, grandma," Kiera said handing over Zoe who nuzzled softly against Elizabeth's shoulder.

"I was young. What else can I say?" Elizabeth answered, a hint of blush rising on her cheeks.

Kiera picked up an envelope and examined the stamp. "Where was he?"

"By this time, he was in England, but when we first started writing, he was in Singapore."

"So, how old was he here?" Kiera nodded to the spray of pages.

"15 or 16, I think. We were about the same age." Elizabeth deciphered the postmark. "This was not long after the moon landing. Such a different time."

"And yet, still just as kinky, it looks like!"

"Some things don't change."

"And boys are boys – always," her daughter smirked.

"Yeah, you've not invented anything new. You've got Me Too now and all sorts of campaigns, but basically nothing's really changed. The boys were always trying something. Girls had to be careful – reputations could be won or lost."

Zoe's small legs stiffened and strained and a sudden aroma hit Elizabeth's nose. She handed her granddaughter back to Kiera.

"I think she needs a change."

Elizabeth pulled the papers together and folded them into their envelope. She placed it back into the box and returned it to its private spot in the sideboard. She was unloading the dishwasher when Kiera returned from changing Zoe's diaper.

"I never realised how many times you had to change them when they're this little," the new mother complained.

"I had no idea how hard it was for previous generations," Elizabeth replied. "When I think my grandmother had to cope with no washing machine or dryer, I wonder how she got it all done. She must have been forever washing clothes. And still she did all the house work and helped with the barn chores. We just have to be glad for what we've got."

"It'll be really different for Zoe," Kiera said watching the baby settle in her arms. "She'll never know what's it like without the internet – unless there's a blackout, of course."

"Oh yes, an age when anyone can know anything at any time! I'm still not sure if that's a good thing or not."

"What about that pen pal of yours?"

Elizabeth jolted at the question. "What do you mean?"

"Well, don't you want to know what happened to him? It's really easy these days to find someone."

"Who says I would want to see him?"

"I'm sorry," Kiera apologised, "maybe he wasn't that important. I had a couple of pen pals—do you remember? They didn't last very long."

"We wrote for several years – much longer than your letters lasted."

"So do you know what became of him?"

"No," Elizabeth admitted sadly, "I think our lives just went different directions. Not that they were actually going in the same way to begin with. We were so far apart."

"It's all there," Kiera said nodding to the laptop lying on the sideboard. "Think I'll put Zoe down for a nap."

Elizabeth tried to change her focus but the urge to fire up the laptop and run a search was growing. Instead she pulled out a chopping board and rustled onions out of their net bag to cut up for the bolognaise sauce that would simmer on the stove top for the rest of the afternoon. She was pouring some red wine onto the browned meat mixture when she heard a car door slam and a creak on the porch to the back door.

"Thought you were working until later," she said to Richard as he bent to smell the contents of the pan. "This won't be ready for quite a while."

"Not a problem," he replied. "I just wanted to see all my best girls."

"You mean you're putting off Blenheim's job until tomorrow," Elizabeth sighed.

"Do you doubt me?" Richard countered with a sliver of a smile poking at the corners of his mouth. "Got a glass of that red to spare?"

An easy hand grazed her waist as Richard squeezed past her to pick a wine glass from the cupboard. A warm cheek touched the side of her face as he briefly kissed her.

"Put her down, Dad," Kiera joked. "There are children present."

"You're old enough," Richard joked. "Where's my very best girl?"

"Just put her down to sleep – you'll have to wait."

"I think that's really why you came home early," Elizabeth challenged. "You just wanted to see Zoe – not the two of us!"

"Busted." Richard pulled out a packet of crackers and found some cheese lurking at the back of the fridge. "Just to keep me going," he explained to Elizabeth's unasked question.

The day fit like a favourite sweater that always folded itself around you in a hug. They sat on the shaded porch, letting Kiera lead the conversation with details of Zoe's first weeks.

Elizabeth made a couple of suggestions over childcare and remembered how her mother had coached her. She was now the matriarch of the family, she realised forlornly, and felt a sudden loss of youthful optimism and a growing resignation to lost time. She took a sip of wine and tried not to let the feeling overwhelm the comfort of the moment.

The bolognaise was nearly ready when Zoe woke up. Richard bounced from his chair on the first little cry and returned with a bundle of baby and blanket. Elizabeth recognised the glow in his face – she had seen it when Kiera was born. He always wanted more children, but it never happened and they learned to be happy with the family they had. Elizabeth could see the yearning had not disappeared but merely lay hidden under the years of day to day life.

28 June 1968

Lizzie could always tell when Sam was interested in a new girl. He became a little bit more buoyant and a little bit louder when he talked, the suppressed excitement igniting the way he spoke. Tonight he had asked to borrow the car for a date with someone new. She was a cousin of one of his friends and had just graduated from the high school in the next district.

The trail of High Karate cologne followed Sam down the hall to his bedroom. He'd spent almost half an hour in the bathroom, making Lizzie nearly bursting from her need to use the room. It was steamy and damp and she rushed out again as quickly as she could. She was surprised to hear her mother's voice coming from her brothers' bedroom as she passed.

"Just make sure you treat her right," Lizzie heard her mother say. Sam's reply was muffled.

"You think I'm interfering?" Another dampened sound from Sam.

"I may be 'old', but I can still remember what it's like when you meet someone special. It's the tingling feeling that's the problem. You can't help it."

"Mom, leave it, would ya?"

"Sam, I'm just saying be careful."

"I've had all the lectures."

"I don't want you getting 'caught', that's all."

"Don't worry – it's not like when you were young."

"Girls still get pregnant."

"Mom, I know. Let it go. It's only a date."

"It's just that I *do* worry. You can't be sure where you'll be in a year's time. You could be..." her voice trailed off.

"Or I could be one year more through college."

"Whatever, you don't need any 'accidents' along the way."

"Message received, Mom."

There was movement by the bedroom door. Lizzie jumped back into the bathroom and pulled the door quietly behind her as her mother whisked along the hall and down the stairs. She was gently pushing the door back open when Sam's head came into view.

"Eavesdropping?"

"Couldn't help it," Lizzie admitted. "Mom's on a mission."

"Yeah, tell me. Don't worry – your turn to get the lecture is coming."

"Not much chance I'll need it." But then the image of Henry's photo crystallised in her thoughts and she hiccupped on a sudden intake of breath.

"You never know," her brother said, retreating into his bedroom for another check in the mirror.

It was nearly midnight when Lizzie heard a soft creak on the stairs as Sam tried to creep past to his bedroom. She had headed upstairs when the 11 o'clock news came on the television. Her mother always waited to see the weather forecast but her father couldn't fight the effect of the early mornings any longer. He had already pushed his dozing frame from his favourite chair and headed to bed. They heard deep snores sounding down the stairs within minutes.

Lizzie lay in the dark waiting for sleep. Johnny was moving around in the boys' bedroom but then it went quiet. The sound of the distant TV was cut off as her mother turned off the lights. She always left one lamp on low just so Sam could see his way through the house. Lizzie knew she was slowing the nightly ritual on the chance of seeing Sam return before she finally settled in bed. An uneasy silence fell over the house until they heard Sam climbing the stairs.

22 June 2018

Elizabeth blamed the wine for her restless sleep. She didn't usually drink that much -- a legacy of an abstemious family – but Richard had encouraged her to have a second glass to go with the spaghetti and a third one carelessly slipped past her lips without her realising it. She hadn't been drunk, but Grandpa Ernest would not have approved regardless, especially as they had a small baby to look after.

She hadn't had her first drink until she was 23. Throughout college there had been offers to try it but she resisted. Friends were slyly snatching drinks before the legal age of 21, and nearly everyone had a drunken night to celebrate their new 'right' to alcohol. But she had always heard the whisper of her mother's disapproval or felt the stern glance of Grandpa Ernest who never had a drop of alcohol during his life.

Even long after she married Richard, she would push the bottles of wine to the back of the cupboard when her parents came to visit. Once her mother saw a half emptied bottle which Elizabeth had used for cooking. The slightest pursing of her lips indicated that she had not approved its use although nothing was said, but she carefully avoided eating the offending sauce when they sat down for the meal.

Elizabeth wasn't sure what woke her at first as she balanced between a dream and her bedroom. The dark figure was about to turn towards her when she was pulled away by wakefulness. Then, she heard the small cry in the next room. There were muffled footsteps and a soft hint of Kiera's voice as she calmed Zoe.

Elizabeth closed her eyes and tried to summon back the enigmatic shapes and feelings of her dream. Richard was not in that darkness. She could feel the warmth of his nearby body and reached out a hand to touch his broad back facing her. There was someone else lingering just beyond consciousness. She willed herself to sleep so she could return to him. A hand stretched out towards her to pull her in and she could feel a soft blackness closing around her.

There was a sharp cry from the next bedroom and the dream fled. Elizabeth lay uneasy in the bed. She stared at the ceiling where shadows from the streetlights filtered through the trees moved with the light breeze. She tossed onto her side just as Richard rolled over on his back. The familiar outline of his face opened up and he started to snore. A flash of anger made her want to shout at him to be quiet. He was stealing her sleep. But, worse, he was preventing her return to the world that was calling her.

A ragged intake of breath turned into a growl ending with a snort. Elizabeth punched her pillow loudly in protest and rolled onto her opposite side to face away from Richard. She tried to claw back the dream, but instead she got a flashback of Henry, peering at her quizzically. She couldn't remember what she had said. He had such beautiful dark eyes, much better than any grainy photograph could have shown. She thought she would be nervous when they first met, but instead it felt like they had always known each other.

Elizabeth squeezed her eyes tight and tried to recall the moments of that meeting, stretching her arms out to embrace the memory. Richard grunted and turned onto his side behind her. A casual arm wound its way around her waist. She stiffened against the intrusion and then softened to let it merge with her reminiscence. As the hand found its customary place around her breast, she remembered her teenage yearnings and let them wash over her.

8 July 1968

      Lizzie was dusted in flour from the efforts to push hair out of her face with the back of her hand. Anna laughed and called her a summer snowman while she scraped a yeasty Dough from a large earthenware bowl onto the floured counter. She began punching and kneading it while Lizzie tried to clean her face.

      Anna's mother had gone out for the day leaving them free to use the large kitchen for one of their baking sessions. Her only request was that the kitchen was clean again by the time she returned. This time they were attempting to master bread making. They had tried once before but the results had been mixed. One loaf of brown bread had been so heavy, Lizzie's mother threatened to use it as a door stop. When they broke it up and spread it out for the birds, even they were reluctant to sample it.

      Lizzie pulled out a second bowl and sucked in the scent of the rising batter. With a grin of pleasure, she stabbed two fingers into the soft Dough and watched as it collapsed in on itself. She teased the mixture onto the prepared counter space and pulled some of the flour onto the sticky mixture.

"It's a great stress release," she said to Anna as she twisted and pummelled the dough.

"Yeah," grunted Anna, her face set with concentration as she kneaded. "What've you got to be stressed about?"

"You know. Still haven't heard if Henry's coming or not. I've lost 5 pounds though!"

"Eating this," Anna waved a hand at the bread rolls that were cooling on the table, "isn't going to help."

"Maybe we should've picked something else to do?"

"Too late now." Anna gave the dough another fierce thwack.

"Hey, don't get carried away," Lizzie warned. "It needs some air in it!"

Anna looked up just as the telephone rang in the next room. She brushed off her hands and wiped them down her apron as she left the kitchen. There was a soft conversation and Lizzie couldn't hear what was being said. Suddenly the handset crashed back onto its cradle and Anna came back into the kitchen. She returned to her station and began cutting the dough to shape into loaves.

"Problem?" Lizzie tried to sound supportive and not nosey.

"Just Eric." There was a harshness in Anna's voice.

"Why's he calling?"

"Ever since that fudgin' hayride," Anna exploded, "he thinks I'm interested in him!"

Anna dropped the dough into the bread tins. Lizzie thought they looked tight and wondered if the loaves would rise.

"Wish I'd never gone that night. Would've been better if you'd been there."

Lizzie felt a momentary pang of guilt. "Well, I just don't fly in those circles, so I couldn't have gone even if we hadn't had the wedding rehearsal."

Lizzie took out a rolling pin and started flattening out her dough into a large rectangle. She concentrated on making it spread evenly. She wanted to ask her friend about that night but was worried what she might learn.

"Can you chop up the nuts for me?" she asked instead.

Anna hacked the nuts to small pieces while Lizzie squished butter, cinnamon and brown sugar with her fingers into a uniform mix. They worked in silence. Lizzie spread the brown sugar and nuts over the rectangle of dough and rolled it up from the side. She sliced the dough log and put circles on a greased pan. Finally, all the bread loaves and rolls were covered and left for a final rise.

They took glasses of iced water onto the porch to wait. The swing creaked as they sat on it.

Lizzie finally spoke, "What happened? You really haven't said much about it."

"That's 'cause I'd rather forget about it. Enough said? Let's talk about something else."

"OK," Lizzie agreed reluctantly. "What movies do you want to see this summer? I don't suppose we can get into see Rosemary's Baby. Johnny went to see it. I don't think he'll admit it, but he got scared!"

"Trouble is that Mrs Winters is on the ticket counter and she *knows* how old we are so we can't fake it!"

"Guess we'll have to wait until we're legal to see it then."

"Demon babies are probably the last thing we need," Anna said. "But I don't like having the seniors gloating about what we haven't seen!"

"Well, they don't even talk to *me*," Lizzie emphasized the last word to point out she felt excluded from Anna's new social circle but her friend wasn't listening.

"Bunch of egotistical pigs, the lot of them. Think they own the world. I thought the girls were bad, but the boys are even worse."

"Hey," Lizzie said sharply, "Johnny was a senior!"

"Yeah, and what's he done for you? You're always complaining about the pranks he's pulling. He's too busy with the other jerks in his class to make any time for you."

"You don't know how brothers work, do ya, since you've never had one of your own!"

"Just seems like you're always upset about something he's done," reasoned Anna.

"Doesn't matter now," Lizzie replied. "He'll be off in September to college and I will be brotherless as well. AND we'll have a new set of seniors in charge."

"Which means Eric will be even more full of himself."

"Come on," begged Lizzie. "What happened that's made you so angry?"

"Just leave it," Anna told her. A timer pinged from inside the house. "Let's get the bread in the oven."

The kitchen was warming up as the bread baked. Wafts of yeast and cinnamon triggered hunger pangs and they escaped back to the porch.

"How many calories do you think are in one of the cinnamon rolls?" Lizzie wanted to know.

"More than you can afford on your diet."

"Not even one?" Lizzie grimaced.

"I warned you and said we could do something else." There was exasperation in Anna's voice.

"I'll work it off riding home," Lizzie countered. "It's not too bad -- not like my birthday coming up. How do I keep from eating then?"

"What're you going to do for it?"

"We're going over to my cousins' for a family get together. But Mom said you could come too if you want, being my best friend and all."

"But, it's all going to be your family?" Anna hesitated. "Don't know if I'd fit in."

"Yeah, but you know most of them already. And Sam's bringing his new girlfriend along. They've only just started going out but, boy, did he get the 'talk' the other night. Mom must think this one is serious. She was lecturing him about 'being careful'. I haven't met her yet but hopefully she will be nicer than the last one."

"Sandy sounded awful," Anna agreed.

"What about it then, coming to my birthday bash?"

"Let me think about," Anna said, "and I'll get back to you.

The smell from the oven spilled out through the screen door. The bread knife and plates were laid out in waiting even before the loaves had been taken out of the oven. Finally, the pans were lifted out and emptied onto the wire racks. Lizzie noted that the loaves were denser than when her mother made bread, but didn't say anything. The cinnamon rolls rose high above the pan and split into delicate shreds when pulled apart. Lizzie couldn't resist the fresh warm rolls which meant the cycle ride home was not long enough to work off calories for two of them.

28 June 2018

It was a couple of days after Kiera and Zoe returned home before Elizabeth had the house all to herself. The nights had been restless with a small baby disturbing the routine. The dream had not come back, but its effect lingered. Memories and emotions from the dream were converging in her mind and taking over any spare corners. They haunted her quiet moments and she was confused in how to interpret them.

She had been thinking about Henry more and more. Until she found the letters, he had been consigned to a distant past and virtually forgotten, but now she couldn't help wondering what had become of him. The 'what ifs' were becoming louder: what if she had stayed longer in England, what if he could have moved to the US, what if they just had more time together – would any of it have changed their relationship.

She couldn't ask herself if she would have been better off marrying Henry instead of Richard. It was a question too far, but yet she could feel it lurking at the edge of reason. Richard had always been more than she expected. She remembered the surprise she felt when he had shown an interest in her when they first met at Gloria and Bill's barbecue. He was tall with broad shoulders. There was an earnestness of conviction when he talked politics, but he had smile creases at the corner of his eyes when he looked at her.

They fit together in a unity that felt good. She always felt safe and loved with him. And now, she thought, it's lapsed into comfort. It was too easy to do the same things every day – 37 years of knowing what will happen next. Three months ago, she thought this was the happiest way to live and now she wondered where the adventure went.

The stack of letters sitting in front of her on the kitchen table taunted her. Even when she was isolated on a farm in a flat expanse of fields and nothingness, Henry had brought excitement, something a little risqué and a glimpse at another life. She opened up the laptop and punched it on. Her fingers tapped the table top nervously as she waited for the computer to boot up. She felt a shiver of sudden anxiety and took a deep breath. She didn't know if finding Henry would aggravate her unrest or puncture the bubble of fantasy building in her head.

She stabbed the icon for the search engine and smiled when a photo of a panda at the National Zoo in Washington flashed up. There was hope she might be pregnant. Everyone wants a baby panda. There had been a lot of false pregnancies. She had gone with Kiera to see the cub born in 2005 who became a star feature at the zoo – adopting poses and looking straight into their camera. Now, it was Zoe who was getting the attention.

Elizabeth resisted the distractions of other news stories and placed the cursor on the search bar. She typed 'Henry Jameson' and pushed the return key. More than 337,000 entries! But, she found, the spelling was slightly wrong on some of the entries and she discarded those. She opened the images gallery to see if she could recognise him there. Historical figures mixed with balding men and a few women, but none of them seemed familiar. None of them had connections to Leeds. She wondered if she would even know him if she saw him. People change over time: old classmates had been unrecognisable at reunions. She found men changed the most with a loss of hair on their heads which seemed to migrate to their faces. At one of the early reunions, a man had stood directly in front of her, challenging her to remember him. She had spent all of her grade school and high school years with him and still didn't know who he was.

When Henry went to university, he was going to study law, but she didn't know if he stayed with it or if he had qualified as a lawyer. If he did, then he would belong to a professional organisation, like the American Bar Association. She googled to find the English equivalent and found the Bar Council website. They called their lawyers barristers. She searched through the information on the home page and clicked on the bar labelled 'Find a Barrister'. This gave her options to go through a 'solicitor' (which she always thought of as a door to door salesman) or through direct access. The latter sounded better but it asked what area of law she needed. She had no idea what type of work Henry could be doing and left the site in exasperation.

Elizabeth didn't know what else to try. She had stayed away from social media and was reluctant to try something she didn't understand. Kiera was always trying to get her onto WhatsApp and Instagram. At one point she had tried Facebook, but she didn't like going onto the pages of people she didn't know.

Before turning off the laptop, she flicked open her Yahoo account to check her Inbox and discovered one of the sporadic emails from Sam. JJ never wrote. She wished she had had a sister. Sisters were for confiding in and support. Brothers just never seemed to get it. She got more news from her sisters-in-law than her brothers but she knew she wasn't a true insider in their lives.

Anna had been the nearest she had ever come to having a sister when they were growing up. She felt a sudden pang of longing for the closeness they had shared. On impulse, she opened a new window and typed Anna Jackson into Google. There were 65 million hits: all the versions of who her friend could be, from doctors and artists to web influencers. It's not surprising, she told herself, with common names like that and her name probably isn't even Jackson any more.

Elizabeth turned back to the list of new emails and brought up the one from Sam.

"Hey, Sis. Hope you're enjoying being a grandparent as much as we have! Can't believe we've got another one on the way. Tell Kiera and Dave congrats from us.

"Was wondering if we could meet up at the farm to have a final sorting out? I've spoken to JJ and he and I could only agree on the one weekend before September : 20-22 July. Know that's your birthday – but any way you could make it? Don't know if you have a party planned or anything – given it's the big 65!! (Wow, how did we get so old?)"

Sam could always make her smile. She wrote a quick reply to say she'd be there. Richard would probably be relieved not to have to organise a celebration for her and have a quiet weekend on his own.

3 July 1968

Dear Mrs Williams,

My name is Henry Jameson. I don't know if you know that Lizzie and I have been pen pals for more than two years now. She has told me a lot about your farm and what it is like to live there. I live in Singapore. It's a big city which must be very different to where you live.

My family is about to make a big change to our lives. We are moving to England in a few weeks. I have never been before, so it will be a huge change for me. We are all excited, but a little nervous as well.

I hope you don't mind my writing to you direct, but I wondered if you could help me surprise Lizzie for her birthday. I would like to call her and actually speak to her for the first time. If I get the difference in time right, I hope to call her in the evening – your time.

Lizzie gave me your telephone number in case we travelled through the United States on our way to England, so I could call from inside the country. But I would like to call her on her birthday instead. I have been earning some money from doing some jobs for pocket money so that I can pay for the call.

I have never made an international call before, so I hope I can book a call with the operator at the right time. I would like to call sometime after 6 pm in Indiana. Could you please make sure she is at home then?

Please don't tell Lizzie about this. I want to surprise her but there is also a chance that I won't be able to get the call through.

Thank you for helping me with this surprise. I hope she has a great birthday.

Regards,
Henry

21 July 1968

Lizzie was unsure whether having her birthday on a Sunday was a good thing or not. On the one hand, it meant that no one was working on the farm apart from doing the necessary daily chores. So everyone could help her celebrate. But it also meant they would have to go to church before any presents were opened.

They had a visiting minister to give the sermon. He was a small gray man who had not visited them before. Lizzie's birthday was mentioned in the announcements and he scanned the congregation searching for the face to accompany the birthday. His eyes settled on her when Johnny held up his index finger pointing at her. Lizzie squirmed in embarrassment and knocked her foot into Johnny's shin when no one was watching. She felt the minister's eyes drift back to her during his lengthy sermon. Lizzie found it difficult to sit thoughtfully as if meditating on what was being said while at the same time trying to remember what she overheard her mother say the night before about a surprise. It was something she wasn't expecting.

There was a sudden silence and Lizzie looked up to see the minister standing back from the pulpit as the organ crashed into the chords of the last hymn. When the congregation streamed out onto the sidewalk, Lizzie struggled through the well-wishers to find Anna waiting for her next to the large maple tree.

"Many happy returns," Anna said holding up a soft wrapped package. "You might need to return this! Wasn't sure on sizes with your new look, and all."

Lizzie fingered the violet ribbon. "Got your stuff?"

Anna held up a canvass bag and said, "All here and ready to go."

"You sounded like you weren't going to come this afternoon."

"You know I've always wanted to see your cousins' place." Anna followed Lizzie back to their car where they waited for the rest of the family.

"Johnny coming?" Anna asked.

"Yeah," Lizzie replied. "And wait 'til you meet Sam's new girlfriend. I think she's the best one yet!"

After a brief stop at the farm to change out of their Sunday best into cooler shorts, the drive to Tom and Barbara's home was about 20 minutes. They had about 30 acres but weren't really farmers. Tom sold insurance around the county. Barbara worked a large vegetable garden and sold produce during the summer at the end of their lane. The twins were sometimes placed on duty near the stall in case anyone passing wanted to buy.

Lizzie thought the best part of their property was the small lake that invited swimmers on searing summer days. A sandy beach wrapped around one side with a dock made from scavenged planks of wood on the opposite side. A rowing boat was tied to an upright post while inflatable rings slowly drifted across the water.

Johnny had been quiet on the drive. The three of them were in the back of the car, with Anna in the middle. Lizzie knew if she sat next to her brother, he would poke her and make fun of her the whole trip but he wouldn't do anything to annoy Anna. Sam and Glenda came in right behind them in the pick-up truck singing along to the new release 'Yellow Submarine.' Sam loved the Beatles.

Laura and Lisa ran out to meet them with two large bouncing, barking German Shepherds at their heels. Anna hesitated getting out of the car, looking warily at the dogs.

"Don't worry," Laura re-assured, "they're friendly, really. Just give 'em a moment to get used to you."

Johnny was already reaching into the fur around the neck of the larger dog, scratching the beast into submission. Lizzie saw him beam his broadest smile at Anna.

"I've got 'em," he told her. "It's safe to come out. I won't let anything happen to you."

Lizzie felt a small pang of jealousy: Johnny would never have showed such courtesy to her but she could see from his smile that Anna was not just his kid sister's best friend any more.

Dan's Rambler lurched up the lane with a cloud of dust spewing out behind. The dogs raced off with new prey in sight, yapping at the car tyres and making the new arrival welcome. When the vehicle came to a stop, Dan jumped out and opened the back door. Simon hesitated before climbing out but was quickly scooped up for a hug by Lizzie's mother. Dan waited for Jackie to turn laboriously in the seat before pulling her gently forward and out of the car.

"Phew," she said, "It's getting harder and harder to move." With a lumbering waddle, she followed the others to the tables erected under a chestnut tree.

"Not much longer now," Lizzie's mother soothed.

"But it's the hardest time," Jackie complained. "And the heat's making it so much worse."

Dan leaned over his wife and carefully stroked her stomach. "Gonna be worth it though, hun."

Lizzie and Anna watched as they loaded Jackie onto a chair with a view down to the lake. They took up places at the far end of the table and waited for the others to sit. Barbara came out of the screen door at the back of the house holding a casserole dish. Charlotte was behind her carrying jugs of lemonade and bubbling about the sights of Yellowstone that they had visited on their honeymoon. Joe carried a tray of glasses and Tom followed with a picnic basket and a cooler.

They were laying out the dishes of potato salad, corn on the cob, fried chicken and baked beans as Grandpa Ernest and Grandma Mary parked their car beside the others. The patriarch of the family added an envelope to the table of birthday presents and took up his place at the head of the table. He loosened the tie worn to church: the suit jacket had been left on the car's back seat. He rolled up his sleeves in deference to the heat.

"Good sermon today," Grandpa Ernest said in a voice matching his name. "Too bad you missed it, Dan."

Lizzie realised she could not recall any of the sermon or even its main point. She hoped Grandpa Ernest didn't turn his attention on her.

"Don't suppose it was about tolerance?" Dan countered across Grandma Mary, sitting between them, who fidgeted with her knife while staring at the lake.

"It was about responsibility," Grandpa Ernest replied. "While God forgives, we have to be responsible for what we do."

"Why don't we eat?" Grandma Mary deflected, knowing from experience how to divert another argument between the father and son. "Can't let the chicken go cold."

Barbara shot her mother a look of relief. Grandpa Ernest bowed his head for the same prayer that Lizzie had heard at every meal throughout her life.

A flurry of dishes were passed. Lizzie found it difficult to stop a big dollop of potato salad ending up on her plate next to two large pieces of deep fried chicken. She closed her mind to the calorie count and willed herself to enjoy her day. The table fell into a calm of eating. The dogs snuffled into people's laps hoping for stray pieces of chicken and Lizzie knew she could pass any excess food off to them without anyone noticing. But the chicken was very tasty, with hints of black pepper sprinkled into the coating, and Lizzie knew very little would 'accidently' fall under the table.

When she had eaten much more than needed to quash any hunger pangs, Lizzie was confronted with the birthday cake. Barbara concentrated on carrying the three layers of chocolate cake carefully from the house to the table. She had spent the previous evening creating roses and bows of icing which she attached to the top and sides. Lizzie thought it nearly looked like a wedding cake with its frills and smiled at the chance to have a piece.

They sang 'Happy Birthday' and Lizzie carved out a section of the cake as her own. Her mother frowned at the size of it and asked, despite it being her birthday, whether she needed that much. Lizzie paused for just a moment and then passed the plate over to Johnny who eagerly claimed it for himself. She hoped her sacrifice would show on the scales.

The family sat back from the dirtied plates and settled into their chairs with iced tea as Lizzie tackled the mound of wrapped items. She started with the package Anna had brought and pulled off the ribbon. She held up a summer blouse and tried to sound grateful as she said thank you, although she could clearly see it was much smaller than she would be able to get into even if the diet worked.

Sam's gift was thin and recognisably a record single, so she was not surprised to find 'Lady Madonna' inside. The plastic encasement had been sliced open. Sam shrugged and grinned in embarrassment.

"Had to make sure it wasn't scratched," he joked while looking at Glenda and laughing over a shared secret.

The envelope from Grandpa Ernest and Grandma Mary held the standard $5 that all grandchildren received. Johnny had wrapped two 10 cent chocolate bars with brown paper and string. She left the parcel from her parents until last and found a selection of books she had asked for. There was no surprise hidden in the presents and Lizzie wondered what her mother had been talking about in the conversation she overheard the night before.

"Mind if I show Anna the shelter?" Lizzie asked Barbara as the adults relaxed into conversation.

"Go ahead," her aunt replied, "the key's on the hook by the back door."

"I'm sure Glenda would like to see it as well," Sam joined in, pulling his girlfriend from the chair.

The four of them took a thin path turning away from the lake to a spot next to the vegetable garden. There was a shed filled with tools and an adjoining door where Lizzie inserted the key. She tugged open the door and flicked the light switch to reveal a long staircase stretching down into the ground.

"C'mon," said Lizzie to her friend. "It's not that scary, really. I've been down a few times."

The air chilled as they descended.

"It's like having air conditioning," Sam put in with his arm around Glenda. "Tell me if you're too cold."

There was a solid concrete door at the base of the stairs sitting on huge hinges. Sam twisted the handle and leaned heavily against the door. Slowly, it began to give way and opened onto a short hallway lined with shelves. Cans of beans, tomatoes and corn sat next to sacks of dehydrated potatoes and powdered milk. There were bottles of water and gas canisters and a shelf stacked with blankets.

"Wow," said Anna. "They really were preparing for the end of the world!"

"It was Tom, mainly," said Sam. "He was scared we'd get into a nuclear war. Especially after the Bay of Pigs episode with Castro. He didn't think it would be so much of a cold war as a hot one! And he wanted to keep them all safe."

They moved into a large room. Camping cots and chairs were folded along one wall. An old couch had been left in the centre with crates of bleach, toilet paper and soap. There was an air of mustiness and abandonment.

"I wouldn't want to stay down here," Glenda said.

"Just as well we may not have to then," Sam told her as he sat on the lumpy couch and gathered her onto his lap. "Although it will do for now."

"Do Tom and Barbara come down here much?" Anna asked.

"I think he used to check every few weeks to make sure the air vents were working and everything was okay." Sam ran a finger along Glenda's shoulder. "Then the countries all started working on a treaty to stop the use of nuclear bombs, so there isn't so much of a threat now. Once that's all signed up, we should all be safe enough."

"That's the educational part of your visit," Lizzie joked, indicating to Anna that they should leave. "Why don't we go to the lake? You can lock up, Sam."

As they emerged from the shelter's door onto the vegetable garden, the heat flattened the goose bumps which had grown on Lizzie's arms in the cool cavern. They could hear shrieks from the direction of the lake. The twins were splashing Johnny who sat in the row boat attempting to manoeuvre it around a circuit.

"Got your swim suit?" Lizzie asked, lifting her T shirt to reveal her own underneath.

"Oh," Anna exclaimed, "you came prepared. Mine's still in the car. You go ahead and I'll meet you down there."

"If you're sure." Lizzie was torn between playing host to her friend and the lure of the water. "There's a bathroom right by the back door you can use."

The twins lay in wait for Lizzie as she approached the beach. Without warning they lunged from behind a bush throwing the contents of their dollar store play buckets over her. Lizzie screamed in surprise.

"You could've at least waited 'til I took off my shorts," she complained although not really angry. She laid out the T shirt and shorts knowing they would dry quickly and raced after the twins who had gone into water. The spring-fed lake sent shockwaves of cold through her body. Johnny's boat came closer and Lizzie grabbed at the oar to try and tip him over. Instead, he dragged it through the water creating a wave that rolled over her. The twins laughed as her hair matted to her head. Lizzie tried cupping her hand to create a spray to repay her brother, but only a few drops reached Johnny. He sat smug on his dry seat and dipped the oars into the water for another tour around the lake.

Lizzie attempted the breast stroke she had learned at summer camp three years before. She wasn't a strong swimmer and didn't like feeling the mud ooze under her feet when she strayed too far from the beachy area. She splashed with the twins and tossed an inflatable ball back and forth with them in the shallow area.

She noticed Johnny was looking past her with a broad smile that engulfed half of his face. He pulled deep on one oar to bring the boat around towards the dock. Lizzie turned to see what he was looking at and caught Anna striding down from the house wearing a bikini she hadn't seen before. The sunlight sparkled on Anna's long golden hair which bounced with each step.

"Come out on the dock," Johnny called over to Anna. "I'll give you a row around the lake."

Anna looked uncertain, looking first at Lizzie, then drawing herself upright and pushing back her shoulders to accent her young curves before turning toward the dock.

Johnny was laughing as he helped Anna into the boat, giving her his hand as she stepped carefully into the middle of the boat. Lizzie noticed his hands were touching Anna's bare arms and back as he positioned her on the seat. There was a flush of pink spreading up Johnny's neck and Lizzie wondered if was from the sun.

The voices grew fainter as the boat moved away from the trio in the shallows. Lizzie walked up the embankment and sat on a large stump which had been carved into a bench. She was surprised Anna had shown any interest in her brother. She never had before, but then Johnny had always treated Anna like a second little sister.

Laura and Lisa were dragging buckets of water out of the lake and dampening the sand to see if they could build a sandcastle. None of them had been to an actual seaside. It was something they saw in magazines, but they had never raced to build a castle against a rising tide.

Across the lake, the two figures in the boat leaned into each other and Lizzie wondered what was being said. They looked too close: intimate, she thought, rolling over the unfamiliar idea in her mind. Lizzie couldn't bear the thought her friend would share secrets with her brother.

The sound of laughter grew louder behind her as Sam and Glenda emerged from the shelter and walked down to the lake. Lizzie noted Sam's shirt had a misaligned button and there was a hint of waxy pink on his jaw which matched the shade of Glenda's lipstick.

"You two swimming?" she asked.

"Not unless it's skinny dipping," Sam said. "Glenda didn't bring a suit."

The twins ran up to throw buckets of water over the new arrivals. The couple shrieked and ran in circles around her to avoid being drenched. Sam caught hold of Lisa and carried her down to the water's edge while Laura hammered on him to release her sister. The battle ended in a huge splash as Lisa was dropped into the water and Sam grabbed Glenda to run back to the house.

Lizzie watched the two out in the boat and, despite the noise, she noted they had not turned back towards the watery fight. She was surprised by their intensity as her own conversations with Johnny usually ended in grunts on his part.

By the time the boat was tied up at the dock, Lizzie could feel the heat of her reddening shoulders. It had been foolish to stay in the sun. She should have found a comfortable place in the shade. Tomorrow the sunburn would feel worse.

"Oh, Lizzie," Anna said as she and Johnny neared, "you need some sun lotion on that!"

"Think I need a drink as well." Lizzie stood up to meet them. "Enjoy the boat?" she asked trying to keep any hint of malice out of her voice.

"Yeah, I was getting the hang of it." Anna replied. "Johnny was showing me how to row. He's pretty good at it."

Johnny drew himself up a little straighter with the praise but uncharacteristically said nothing. Lizzie shot him a glare, but he wasn't looking at her and it missed its mark.

"C'mon, girls," she said instead to the twins. "Let's all see if we can find some drinks. And," she said under her breath, "maybe some more cake."

When they arrived back at the table, Sam and Glenda were looking sullen. There was a tenseness in the air that Lizzie did not understand. Her father was talking in stilted sentences about how the baling was progressing and the women were listening to Charlotte lament about the long drive back from Yellowstone.   Joe hovered nearby, mindlessly stroking Charlotte's arm during the story.

Lizzie and Anna flopped onto their chairs .

"You've overdone it in the sun, Lizzie," her mother said as she passed the jug of lemonade. "I've got some cream at home. It's time we were going anyway."

"Jackie," said Grandma Mary, "we can take you home."

"Where's Uncle Dan?" Lizzie asked realising suddenly that he was missing.

There was a terse pause when no one spoke. Lizzie looked from her mother to her father, confused by the silence.

"He left earlier," her mother said eventually.

"And left Jackie and Simon?" Lizzie looked around the circle of faces for an answer.

There was a long pause before Grandpa Ernest spoke.

"He shouldn't have said what he did," he humphed.

"Why, what was that?"

"Just leave it for now, Lizzie," her mother directed.

Lizzie noticed a slight reddening at the edges of Jackie's eyes and wondered if she had been crying. Simon played with some toy cars oblivious to any disharmony among the adults.

A plume of dust rose over the lane and the Rambler spun into view. Dan pulled it up sharply at an angle to the other cars and swung open his door. He tumbled out and held the car frame to steady himself.

Everyone watched as he swayed left and right while walking to the table.

"Jackie," he shouted. "Time to go. You's ready?"

Jackie put her hand on the arm of the chair to hoist herself up, but Grandpa Ernest motioned for her to stay seated. Although everything around the table seemed highly charged, Lizzie felt a tremendous stillness coming from her grandfather.

"We'll take her," he told Dan.

"I came," Dan leered, "to get her. It's time to go home."

"She will be safer with us."

"What d'you mean, safer? I wouldn't hurt her."

"You're not fit to drive, at the moment," Grandpa Ernest said. The teenagers sat frozen in their chairs. No one ever challenged Grandpa Ernest.

"Why? 'Cause I had a beer or two?" Dan argued. "You don't like drinking, do you? God say you can't drink?"

Grandpa Ernest half closed his eyes. Lizzie saw a twitch along his jaw line where the muscles tensed. He spoke softly with a hardness Lizzie had never heard before.

"I do not want to hear your jokes about my church. Isn't it bad enough that you come here drunk against everything that I raised you to be? I will not have you in this family if you cannot show respect."

"Jackie," Dan called again.

"I said we will take her and Simon home," Grandpa Ernest said dismissing Dan by turning his back to him. Jackie shook her head and Dan retreated back to his car. The engine revved and the wheels slid on the gravel as he raced back down the lane.

The family sat, unsure what could be said. Finally, Sam broke the void saying he needed to take Glenda home before evening chores and there was an embarrassed busyness as plates and bowls were cleared and the table emptied. Lizzie gathered the remains of her birthday gifts into a bag as Charlotte gave her a hug and told her to enjoy the rest of her day.

The ride home was stretched by silence. Anna fit awkwardly back into her seat between Lizzie and Johnny, but there was no banter. Lizzie stared out the window and tried to hide her disappointment. It was meant to be her special day.

They dropped off Anna in town before the men changed into work clothes and headed out for the milking. Lizzie's mother searched around the kitchen for something to cook for supper, opening cabinet doors, staring inside and then listlessly closing them again. She glanced at the clock and quietly lifted the telephone receiver to hear the dial tone.

Lizzie picked up the copy of the last Look magazine and thumbed through the pages. The cover title read *The American Dream is not Dead*. Inside, she found nine pages of rural life. Was this the dream, she wondered, feeling more that she had been stranded in some back water while the main river of life had taken another direction. She flicked the pages and came to the last photos of Robert Kennedy before he died. She skimmed past *It's OK to Cry in the Office*. She already felt despondent after what she would call her non-birthday and didn't want to know that her future working life might not be any happier.

Lizzie glanced at the coffee table and the TV Guide which arrived every week in the mail. It was Sunday evening and ever since she could remember they had always watched the Ed Sullivan show. There wasn't any point in looking to see what else was on.

The phone rang and Lizzie jumped to get it while her mother hovered nearby.

"Oh, hi, Grandma."

"I hope you're enjoying your birthday. How's the sunburn?"

"Warm," said Lizzie. "Wish I had sat in the shade. Mum's put lotion on it though...."

"Is your mother there?" Grandma Mary cut in. "I'd like a word."

Lizzie passed over the handset to her mother and went to sit on the porch to hope for something interesting to watch drive down the road. She could hear the rise and fall of her mother's voice, but not the words. The regular pump of the milking machine stopped. Her dad and brothers would be in for supper in twenty minutes.

"Lizzie," her mother called. "Come and give me a hand."

They were stacking a variety of sandwiches on plates when the men came in. Her mother apologised for the simple meal, but said she needed to go to the store. After eating, Lizzie helped wash up the dishes before settling in front the television with the rest of the family. She tried to suggest that they could go out for ice cream. She felt the need to offset the day's disaster with a caramel sundae, but her mother said no one else felt like going. So instead, Lizzie slumped into the overstuffed chair with her chin buried in her chest waiting for bedtime and willing the day to end.

Her father watched the first two acts on the Ed Sullivan show before heavy rumbling started to come from his end of the couch. Her mother kept getting up to get a drink of water or a tissue. As she passed the telephone, she would quietly lift the handset to check for a dial tone.

Finally, Lizzie surrendered and headed to bed. Her brothers said goodnight but no one mentioned her birthday. She felt as if it had never happened.

23 July 1968

Dear Mrs. Williams,

Can I first of all apologise for not calling on Lizzie's birthday. I really meant to call and I had booked it with the operator, but something happened on the day before which meant I couldn't call. I hope she had a very good birthday all the same.

The difference in time meant I was going to call in the morning my time yesterday, which would have been after 6 pm your time. But my sister Susan was in a car accident late on Sunday night. We were at the hospital most of the night. We were really worried because it was a very bad crash. I am glad to say though that she escaped with just a broken leg. Her friend who was driving will be in the hospital longer, but is expected to recover fully as well.

So, as you can guess we were all thinking about Susan and the call to Lizzie got forgotten. I hope you didn't tell her about it or she would be disappointed (I hope).

I am sorry to have troubled you as the call did not happen, but thank you for keeping this secret. Maybe someday we will meet.

Regards,
Henry

14 July 2018

The card was hidden behind a large folder wedged at the base of the box. Elizabeth had missed it when she poured out Henry's letters. She had wanted to look through them once again for clues about what might have become of him. She wondered what was in the folder but it fit tightly inside the box. She tried to prise it out with her fingernail, but the nail split and tore. Sucking the wounded finger, she reached for a table knife and slid it down a corner to lever out the folder.

A couple of old school report cards fell out of the folder and Elizabeth remembered the embarrassment she had felt in getting that 'D' in Algebra. Even now, she felt confused as to how it happened. It was in her sophomore year. She had been pretty good in maths, getting mostly 'A's with occasional 'B's up until that point. Anna had been her competition. Anna could write better reports and excelled in science, but Elizabeth matched her in maths. They battled to see who could get the better scores on their tests. All throughout grade school, it had always been one of them who had the top test results. No one else in their class ever beat them. Elizabeth felt a pang of loss as she suddenly remembered this was the year Anna had left.

Elizabeth was about to close the lid on the box when she noticed the two envelopes. She recognised Henry's handwriting, but then realised that the letters were not addressed to her. When had Henry written to her mother? She couldn't remember seeing these letters before, but they were in her box. She opened the white envelope that clearly held a card. He apologised for NOT calling her on her birthday? The blue aerogram written to her mother explained he was intending to surprise her with a telephone call. She couldn't remember her mother telling her about this. Elizabeth must have seen the letters

– they were in her box - but it felt more like a newly discovered secret. She was torn between wondering why her mother had never told her and being overwhelmed by the gesture itself. Would she even have known at 15 how to make an international call? They didn't know anyone who lived outside of the country. No one she knew then had ever called internationally before. It wasn't the same as now, she thought. There was no Skype or direct dialling.

When she was a student in France, she had to arrange a time to call home and book it through an operator. She had sat in a draughty corridor waiting nervously for a ring on the heavy black phone fixed to the wall. The operator became easier to understand the longer she lived in Paris, but the first couple of calls had been extremely difficult as she practised her American accented French. The operator would check she was there and then call their number in Indiana and ask for her parents. She was relieved when finally she heard her mother's voice, despite sounding tinny and echoing on the international cable.

But she was older then, not 15.

What had he become, this boy with so much promise? She wondered if he remembered her at all. She had locked away that time of her life in memories that were rarely used and left his letters forgotten. Had he done the same or would he remember her if she showed up on his doorstep?

She rifled through the cascade of letters to check the postmarks for the later letters in the hope that they might help to link him to the present. The inked marks were difficult to read. Some were partially missing or the date was stamped over a distracting image. Finally, she decided that a letter from September 1974 was the last one she received.

It was a simple white envelope with her name and address. There were no embellishments of stickers or 'SWAK' or last minute thoughts on the back. The writing was widely spaced as if to fill the pages but say as little as possible. It was so different from those earlier letters where every inch was crowded with words and drawings.

He apologised for the delay in replying but his father had been very ill. In fact, the doctors were not sure how long he might live. It had been hard on the family and he had dropped out of university for the moment to be with them. She noted that he was still at his parents' address in Leeds. He was thinking of transferring his course to Leeds University so he could live at home and help his family. It would save money as well and with his father not being able to work, there were financial pressures. He wished her well and hoped she would be successful in her own degree course.

Elizabeth turned the page over and stared at its blankness. She felt a distance leaking from it, pushing her away into her separate future. Without saying goodbye, the letter had become an ending. She was hollowed out by the words, a peculiar emptiness taking over her curiosity. Slowly, she gathered the letters into the box and returned it to its space in the sideboard.

22 July 1968

The day after her birthday, the mood at breakfast was still muted. The warmth from the oven made the air heavy with heat. Lizzie's mother had been up early kneading and proving loaves of bread to bake before the temperature rose too high. It was going to be another hot day.

Johnny grinned at Lizzie as she sat down just in time for her father to give the blessing over the meal. Lizzie scowled back, still cross that Anna had spent more time with him than her yesterday.

Her mother plated up sausage patties and fried eggs and put them on the table. Johnny went to stab a sausage with his fork but was stopped by their mother.

"Just wait," she said irritably, "until it's passed to you. Can't have you just taking whatever you want."

John Sr picked up the platter and slid two eggs and patties onto his plate before handing it to Sam to take his breakfast. The platter next went to Lizzie who passed it, with only one egg remaining, to Johnny with a smirk.

"I'm a growing boy," he complained as he scraped off the remains onto his plate.

"Leave some for your mother," John Sr ordered.

"No," she said, "I'm not very hungry. I'll just have cereal."

John Sr frowned at his namesake and Johnny knew not to ask for more.

The radio filled the gaps between the clink of bowls and the scraping of plates. No one spoke while the DJ gave the weather forecast and the music turned into news.

The phone rang as the farm jobs were being handed out to Johnny and Sam. Lizzie's mother jumped to answer it before the third ring. She kept her voice low. Lizzie couldn't hear what she was saying and was distracted by 'Yummy, yummy, yummy, I got love in my tummy,' playing on the radio. She was singing along quietly when her mother came back to the table.

"That was your mother." Lizzie's mother said to her husband, giving one of what Lizzie called her 'meaningful' looks. "They'd like to talk to us this morning."

"Really?" her father said with some frustration. "I've got to get up to the fields...."

"It's what your parents want. They stressed *now*." The corner of her mother's mouth tightened. Her eyes darted over Johnny and Sam before returning to hold her husband's gaze.

"Alright," John Sr broke their soundless conversation and looked toward Sam. "You and Johnny get the wagons ready and start on the north field. I'll be back as fast as I can."

Lizzie was surprised he was leaving her brothers to get on with the job. Nothing usually came before the day's task list. It was a clear hot day, perfect for baling and she would have expected them to work a long day to get as much done as possible.

Johnny grabbed another piece of toast as their parents pushed back their chairs.

"Lizzie," her mother directed, "after you've cleaned up the kitchen, get started on picking the green beans. We'll process them this afternoon."

Lizzie had not even finished filling the sink with soapy water to scrub the dishes when the door slammed and her parents were gone.

"What d'ya think that's about?" Johnny said through the bread circling in his mouth.

"Something about yesterday, I suppose," Sam shrugged. "They were really strange when Glenda and I went back to the table. No one said much. Doesn't seem they want to tell us what it's about either."

"It was *such* a fun day anyway," Lizzie moaned sarcastically under her breath.

"What d'ya say?" Johnny asked.

"Oh, just go and leave me alone," Lizzie told him, wanting to be left to wallow in the ashes of her spoiled day.

The day was warming fast when she headed to the vegetable garden. She covered up with a loose, long sleeved shirt to protect her bright pink shoulders. She didn't like anything rubbing against the sunburn, but she couldn't risk making it worse. The lotion her mother had put on the night before had been soothing, but she felt her skin tighten every time she reached for another handful of beans.

She could hear the tractor in the distance as a faint rumble that faded in and out as it moved up and down the field. The second basket was almost filled with beans when she saw the dust flying up behind the postman's van. She thought Henry might send her a card for her birthday, but none had come so far. Maybe, she hoped, it would be in today's mail.

It was nearly noon as she walked down the lane to the mailbox and the mercury on the thermometer was already at 83 degrees. She could feel the drops of sweat forming and rolling down her back and wished she had settled in the shade instead.

The flap on the mailbox was slightly ajar. The mailman had pushed the selection of newspapers, flyers and letters in as far as possible, but it still wouldn't close completely. Lizzie tugged the papers out and flicked through the envelopes. The neighbour's son, Steve, honked as he raced by in a spray of gravel and dirt, but she barely looked up. It was quickly clear there were no foreign letters. Lizzie curled the newspapers around the smaller items and wedged it under her arm for the hike back to the house.

Sam and Johnny sat on the porch waiting for her. They were red faced and covered in chaff from haymaking. Two emptied water glasses sat on the table between them.

"It's lunchtime," Johnny answered to an unasked question.

"They're not back yet," Lizzie responded pushing past into the shade of the house. She shoved the bundle of mail onto her father's desk and headed to the kitchen to rummage ingredients for a meal. She washed and snapped some of the beans she had picked during the morning and set them on the heat to cook. The pan of water was just coming to a boil for pasta when she heard the back door crash against the wall announcing the return of her parents.

Her mother assessed the pans on the stove and nodded approval. She started to pull leftover pieces of meat from the refrigerator and sliced some of their juicy garden ripened tomatoes. Together they worked to make a sauce for the pasta.

"Did you get the mail, Lizzie? It wasn't down there," her father called.

"On your desk," she called as she poured the cooked pasta into the sauce and stirred to combine them.

Sam and Johnny were seated at the table, eager to eat, when John Sr came into the kitchen carrying the collection of mail.

"This," he said solemnly handing an official looking envelope to Sam, "is for you."

Her mother looked up at that moment and Lizzie heard a catch in her breath. They all watched as Sam cautiously pealed back the gummed flap and pulled out the form letter on which his name and address had been typed.

"Hey, the President is writing to you!" Johnny said looking over his shoulder.

"Yeah, he wants me to visit, possibly for a long stay."

"No, no," her mother whimpered. "You can't go."

"Uncle Sam wants Sam!" Johnny joked, but no one laughed.

The draft notice was passed around the table: "You are hereby ordered for induction into the Armed Forces of the United States." Bring your social security number, Lizzie read. Bring details of any life insurance policy. Bring clothes for 3 days and money for a month to buy personal items. A chill passed down Lizzie's spine. He really could be sent to fight in the war.

"7 am?" Johnny shouted. "That's really early. Guess they like farm boys that get up for milking!"

"When do you go?" their mother choked back tears.

"Not until the 6th of August," Sam told her.

"So soon?"

"Look," their father said as he read through the notice, "it says you 'may be found NOT qualified for induction'."

"Fred O'Neill still hasn't been found..." her mother's voice faded into fear. She had visited his family regularly since it was reported that Fred had disappeared while fighting in Vietnam.

"Nothing we can do at the moment," John Sr said pragmatically. "We'll just have to wait and see what the draft board says on the day."

Lizzie found it hard to think of anything else as they tried to eat their lunch, yet none of them were able to talk about it. There were stifled sniffs from her mother and Lizzie noticed a reddening around her eyes. Her father was solid and calm, as always, but there was a sharpness in his voice as he asked Sam and Johnny about how far they had gotten with the baling in the morning.

After the meal, her brothers waited outside to get started on the afternoon's work. Lizzie flicked through the flyers that had come with the mail to see if there were any good offers at local stores while her mother stood with her hands in the sink scrubbing the plates and blindly staring out the window at the countryside. Her father slid an arm across her mother's shoulders and she leaned into him.

"Let's not worry 'til we have to," he told her.

"I know," she replied quietly. "What'll we do about Dan?"

"I think we have enough of our own problems." He squeezed her gently. "He's going to have to deal with Dad on his own. I can't help. Don't know that I would want to anyway."

The surprise of the draft notice had distracted them from the morning's drama and Lizzie realised no one had said anything about their visit to see Grandpa Ernest and Grandma Mary. She was about to ask her mother about it after her father had left to join Sam and Johnny, when she was sent to collect the baskets of beans she had picked during the morning.

As they spread out newspapers and pans in the living room, Elizabeth tried again to ask why they had visited the grandparents, but her mother shushed her in mid-question and feigned interest in what was on the television. They spent a rare afternoon focussed on the daytime soap opera 'Days of Our Lives', as they snapped ends off of the beans, preparing them to be blanched and frozen for the winter.

21 July 2018

They wanted to get started early on the second day of the clear out, but Sam had suggested having breakfast at a diner in Fenton which they used to visit when they were children. The menu was still the same, but the owners had moved two generations down the family. By the time the strawberry waffles and third cups of coffee were finished, they were too full to move quickly.

"Happy Birthday, Sis," Sam said to Elizabeth, raising the last of his orange juice as a toast.

"Yeah, great day for it," JJ added and then thought. "What is it now? Ouch – 65!"

"As if I need reminding," Elizabeth said glumly. "Sometimes you just want to forget all about it."

"You can't help but remember when you're going through all the stuff in the house." Sam settled back in his seat. "Mom must've kept every scrap of paper she ever touched!"

The day before, they had emptied cupboards and drawers and sifted through their contents. Mementoes were put to one side and the bulk of their parents' redundant history was taken along narrow trails through the debris to the dumpster which had been hired for the weekend.

"I think I found every science project I ever worked on," JJ said. "Wish I'd gotten better grades on them."

"I was looking through the photos I took home when I was here last time." Elizabeth pulled the group photo from Charlotte's wedding out of her handbag. "You know, I think this is the last picture of the whole family with Grandpa Ernest and Grandma Mary."

"Yeah, look how young we are there!" JJ whistled. "What year was this?"

"1968."

"Oh, yeah. I'd just graduated high school. And you," JJ turned to Sam, "were on girlfriend 87 already."

"Wasn't as bad as that," Sam countered.

"Can you remember who it was that summer, then?" JJ challenged.

"Pity about Charlotte," said Elizabeth. " It would have been their 50th anniversary this year. I should go see Joe at Merry Woods before we head home. Last I heard, he was doing well there. Apparently, he's still very good at bridge and he's got lots of people to play with."

"That makes Sandy 50 this year then." JJ pointed at the photo. "See how big Aunt Jackie is here."

"Vicky. It was Vicky," Sam mused through his memories.

"Naw, that was after I went to college," JJ said. "I remember coming home for Thanksgiving and she was here."

"Have you seen Sandy or Simon lately?" Elizabeth put the photo back in her handbag.

"Saw Sandy on Facebook," said JJ. "The oldest girls are in college and the other two are in high school. Jackie moved near her some years back to help with the kids."

"Gloria?"

"She was *your* girlfriend, Sam: you should know," JJ cajoled. "Getting forgetful or just too many girls? Better be the former, for Julia's sake."

"There've been no other women since Julia and I got married."

"Mom would have been pleased about that," Elizabeth joked. "She was always worried about you leaving a trail of 'responsibilities'!"

JJ was assigned the barn and sheds to make an inventory of any machinery and decide what tools he wanted to keep. The tool shed had been one of JJ's favourite haunts when he was younger and led to his interest in running his own hardware store. When he settled in Vermont, their parents' hopes for someone to take over the farm were destroyed. Sam had already trained as an architect and moved to Oregon and there was never any expectation that Elizabeth would become a farmer.

Sam and Elizabeth were assessing the house contents, when her cell phone rang.

"Happy birthday," Richard sang. "Hope it's going well."

"Just so much stuff," Elizabeth complained. "Not much of a fun birthday."

"Sorry about that," her husband commiserated. "I do have a present for you though. It should be arriving this afternoon."

"Won't be much of a present for me here!" Elizabeth felt aggrieved suddenly that she was missing out on her celebrations.

"No," Richard said, "it's coming to you. I've hired a company to transport your Dad's desk back to us. You said you wanted to keep it and Sam and JJ said it was fine with them."

Elizabeth looked up to see Sam smiling broadly.

"You did that?" She was shaken by the unexpected thoughtful gesture

"I'll take you out to celebrate properly when you're back," Richard promised. "Just don't party too much without me."

"Not a lot of danger of that," Elizabeth replied before ending the call.

"What?" said Sam, "Don't you think we can party in Indiana?"

Elizabeth gave him an exaggerated frown. "Certainly won't be popping any corks, now will I?"

"I'd be up for that," Sam replied, "but you know JJ. He wouldn't like it. How he ended up being the one most like Dad, I don't understand. Maybe it's because he was named for him?"

"Think he wanted the desk?" Elizabeth asked.

"No, he said he didn't have room. I did check before giving the okay."

The double pedestal oak desk sat in an alcove overlooking the southern fields. It had been an unmoving fixture throughout their lives where their father reviewed the farm accounts, made job lists, paid bills and sometimes just sat looking over the wide expanse of his farm. Elizabeth told Richard she had always loved it as a beautiful piece of furniture, but she knew it was the anchor to the past that she wanted even more.

The moving van arrived mid-afternoon. Sam helped the driver lift the desk from its spot and heft in through the tight doorway to load it onto the vehicle. Four indentations in the carpet were all that remained of its decades by the window.

"It'll probably get there before me," Elizabeth said as the van disappeared down the road. "Even if it's taking the road and I'm not!"

"The room really looks strange without it," JJ said coming up behind her.

"I don't know if I want to see the house when it's empty," Elizabeth said. "Doesn't feel right at all."

"I know," Sam agreed, "but it needs to be cleared for the sale. What're you taking, JJ?"

"I've sorted out some of Dad's tools, which is why I drove the pick-up. Everything else is ready for the auctioneer. Barb says she'd like the wall cabinet for our dining room if no one else wants it."

Elizabeth was pleased they could agree on what each of them would keep. She had heard too many stories of families falling out over their parents' legacies with arguments turning to feuds. She never wanted that to happen to them.

As the afternoon turned into evening, they called a halt for the day. Elizabeth felt tired and hungry. She'd forgotten it was her birthday until Sam pulled out some lawn chairs and directed her to the barren patch that had once been their vegetable garden. While she and Sam had been busy inside the house, JJ had collected old wooden crates, logs, papers and anything that would burn into a large heap.

Elizabeth laughed as JJ went to light the bonfire. "Just don't try and light it like Dad – with gasoline!"

As far back as she could remember, there had always been at least one summer bonfire with family and friends. Her father sat near the fire whittling sharp points onto freshly cut long sticks, handing them out as they were completed. A longer stick meant some escape from the fierce heat of the fire when cooking the hot dog implanted on the stick's end. Her mother provided the buns and accompaniments of ketchup, mustard and relishes. There were also steaming piles of corn on the cob and bowls of potato salad. The feast would be finished with marshmallows roasted over the reducing flames.

Elizabeth sat back in the chair letting the glow of the fire rekindle happy memories. Sam pulled up a cooler beside her, took out a bottle of cold lemonade and handed it to her. He grabbed a long stick propped against a chair and reached back into the box. Suddenly, Elizabeth was face to face with a hot dog on a stick.

"Ready to go," Sam said holding out the stick to her. "Thought this might be the best way to celebrate your birthday."

"Our last bonfire," JJ commiserated. "Hopefully, not your last birthday, though!"

It was later, after they ate blistered hot dogs, ears of corn wrapped in foil and roasted in the fire and potato salad from supermarket tubs, that Elizabeth relaxed in her chair with a hint of sticky marshmallow on the edge of her lips.

"This was a much better birthday than 50 years ago," she sighed. "Thank you."

"Don't think I remember that one," Sam said.

"Oh," Elizabeth explained, "I always thought it was my worst birthday – ever. Do you remember? We were at Barbara and Tom's. My friend Anna was there and you had your girlfriend...."

"Glenda!!" Sam exploded. "That was her name."

"What was so bad?" JJ said. "I remember having a good time at the lake."

"*You* did," Elizabeth still felt a trace of resentment, "because you took Anna out on the lake for ages. Sam was off making out with Glenda and I got left with the twins."

"You really hold a grudge," Sam said.

"It was *my* birthday." Elizabeth realised she had never let her disappointment go. "Anna was my friend, but you monopolised her. And then the family was weird with Dan. That seemed to be the day when they all fell out. It was the first time I ever saw Dan drunk."

"Not the last time, unfortunately," Sam added.

"I remember Anna," JJ put in. "She was really cute. Fantastic hair. Blonde. I really would've liked to date her, but she was too young. And she was my kid sister's friend...."

"But you were talking to her for ages!"

"It was one of the few heart to hearts I had had with a girl at that point. I was surprised she wanted to talk to me, but she had a problem she thought I could help with."

"What could you possibly have given advice on?" Elizabeth doubted.

"Something," JJ tried to remember, "to do with an older guy that she was having problems with. Think one of the seniors must've been giving her problems. I don't know - it's too long ago to remember just what it was about. Seemed important to her, is all I can recall."

"I thought you wanted to go out with her."

"Sam would probably have gotten to her before I did," JJ laughed.

"Right. Where do I find her? Maybe she's still a catch," Sam joked.

"Her family moved away a few months later. Never heard from her again," Elizabeth said with some bitterness. "She didn't even tell me where they were going."

"Why'd they move? " Sam asked.

"Said her dad got a new job," Elizabeth answered feeling a sudden confusion she did not understand.

"Saw her once," JJ said as he tried to pick bits of corn from between his teeth

"Really? When?" Elizabeth wanted to know.

"It wasn't long after the shopping mall opened. What was that, back in mid or late 70s? I took Grandma Mary in to have a look at it. I went off to a menswear store and left Grandma sitting on a bench in the central area. When I came back, Anna was talking to her. I recognised her by the hair – she was still really good looking."

"Did she say where she lived?"

JJ paused while he thought. "Somewhere south. I think near the Ohio River, but I'm not sure where."

"What were they talking about?"

"Oh, just saying hello, really. She knew Grandma from church and, of course, she was our grandma."

"But why was she there?"

"You're asking me after 40 years?" JJ challenged. "I imagine she was visiting family and went to see the new mall like we all did when we visited."

"Just don't understand why she didn't come see me," Elizabeth sighed.

"You weren't living there then," JJ said dismissively. "We'd all moved away. She probably didn't expect you to be around anyway."

"I suppose so." She was surprised to still feel the shadow of lost friendship. "No one ever mentioned they had seen her."

"You're going to have to let it go," Sam told her. "It's too long ago to worry about."

Elizabeth knew he was right but her mind kept going back to her last few weeks with Anna, picking over the moments like pulling at a scab that hadn't fully healed. When Anna told her they were moving, she hadn't believed it at first. She thought it was a joke that Anna had dreamed up with Johnny because Elizabeth had been so irritable after her miserable birthday. It was a few weeks later as she saw Anna and her mother loading boxes with plates and vases that she actually believed they would go.

"You haven't mentioned Anna for years," Sam went on. "Why such interest now? It was a long time ago."

"Just a bit of a nostalgia trip, I guess," Elizabeth admitted. "Found some old letters the last time I was here. Took me right back to that summer."

"What letters?" JJ sat down with yet another marshmallow toasted golden in the bonfire embers.

"From my pen pal?"

Her brothers stared at her blankly.

"I had a pen pal in Singapore. Well, that summer he wrote he was moving to England. I'd left all the letters up in a box with my other stuff and it was still there when we were clearing out."

"Kind of a secret boyfriend then?" JJ chided.

Elizabeth hesitated, feeling an impossible blush creeping over her ears as she tried to avoid admitting the emotions that accompanied the letters.

"Course he wasn't," she said more loudly than needed. "Hadn't met him. But we liked writing to each other."

"What became of him, then?" the practical Sam asked.

"We lost touch, years later." Elizabeth shifted in the chair. "He wanted to be a lawyer, but I don't know if that's what he did."

"Did you know," Sam deviated, "lawyers in England are called 'Solicitors'? How's that for division by a common language? You'd think they were giving out legal advice on the doorstep!"

"I thought they were called barristers," Elizabeth said.

"No," JJ interjected, "don't they make coffee?"

Elizabeth scowled at him, "Not baristas."

"Had an English client once," Sam continued, "and when we did the contracts, he had his 'Solicitor' go over everything. Think he said that barristers go to court. Don't remember for sure: it was a few years ago."

Elizabeth picked up her lemonade bottle and used paper plate and stuffed them into the cooler. "Well, I suppose it doesn't matter, anyway. It was a long time ago."

They sat staring into the embers while the fireflies began to rise from the damp grass. The sky gradually darkened into night and the spray of the Milky Way spread out over their heads. The croaking frogs sounded just as they had 50 years before.

25th July 1968

    The church committee met on Thursday evenings. Grandpa Ernest had been a member for more than 20 years and taken the roles of treasurer and chairman at different times. He was using his experience to train John Sr to take on the responsibility of caring for the wellbeing of the church and its congregation. With nearly half of the town belonging to the church, leading the committee was a position of respect within the community and something Grandpa Ernest accepted with considerable gravity.

    It was always a race to complete the milking in time when Lizzie's father had an evening meeting. Tonight he started the milking a little bit earlier so he would have time to eat supper and clean up before going to the meeting at 8 pm. He came out of the bathroom after a quick shower in a waft of Old Spice cologne, the smell of the milking parlour completely banished.

    Lizzie's mother was joining the women's sewing group which was held at the same time in the church basement where Charlotte and Joe held their wedding reception. Instead of tiers of cake and swags of crepe paper decorations, the tables were laid with bolts of fabric and patches which had been cut and were waiting to be stitched together. They were making quilts for tornado victims in Iowa and Arkansas. They had been sending help since May when the disaster struck. Two committee members had driven trailer loads of second hand clothes, household items and food to the area to help the hundreds who lost their homes. As the quilts wouldn't be needed until the weather turned cooler, the ladies of the church had time to sew their hearts into each seam while wishing no one would ever need to do the same for them.

Lizzie followed her parents to the car as Sam got into the pickup truck for a date with Glenda.

"Can you drop me at Anna's? She said to come by if I could."

Her father waved Lizzie into the back seat and they sped down the lane and into town. Anna had been keeping watch for her and the door was already open when Lizzie walked up to the porch.

"You feeling older and wiser?" Anna smirked.

"Thanks for that," Lizzie replied settling into the wicker chair on the porch. "I was trying to forget Sunday."

"Hey, it was fun on the lake."

"If you say so. You went off and left me with the twins," Lizzie complained. "I thought you'd had enough of seniors."

"Which is why I needed some 'brotherly' advice," Anna said. "He just wasn't *my* brother."

"Can't believe he could say anything useful," Lizzie grumped.

"Oh well, if you're going to carry on like that, I just might move away!"

"Yeah, well," said Lizzie, "you can take Johnny with you, if you like."

"Anyway, thanks for the loan of your brother. I'm sorry if that upset you."

"It was just a strange birthday. Hopefully they'll be better in the future."

Anna changed the subject. "How's the diet going?"

"Well, I lost about 5 pounds, but I've been worried so much this week, I can't stop eating." Lizzie told her. Anna lifted her eyebrows as a question. "Sam's got his draft notice. We're all out of our minds, worried he'll get taken in."

"Have you told your parents yet about Henry coming?"

"No," Lizzie said. "And I can't now. Everyone's bummed about Sam."

"What if he turns up?" Anna insisted.

"I'm almost hoping he won't," admitted Lizzie. "It's crazy because I'd like to meet him, but I am scared what might happen."

Anna was silent. They watched as the sun settled in an orange glow on the horizon behind a large maple tree. Long purple shadows snaked towards them across the street. They let the evening turn into darkness while they talked about their current favourite TV shows. A pair of headlights appeared down the road. The twin lights swayed left and right across the road as if dancing to an unheard melody.

"What's it doing?" Anna said standing up. "They're gonna crash if they go on like that."

They watched as the lights came closer and slid sideways to a halt beside Anna's mailbox. Against the brightness of the headlamps, Lizzie saw the driver's door open and a dark figure lurch onto the sidewalk.

"What 'cha doing?" Lizzie recognised the slurred voice of her uncle.

"Dan," she called to him. "Go home. Have some coffee."

"Ah, Lizzie," the voice came back. "my favourite niece. Well, my oldest niece."

"What are you doing here?" Lizzie shouted to him. Their raised voices had brought Anna's parents out onto the porch.

"Just going…." Came the slow reply, "home." Dan stumbled against the car.

Lizzie shifted on her foot, about to run down the path to help him, but Anna's father held out an arm to stop her.

"Stay here," he said. "It's safer. I'll see he gets home."

Anna's father strode over to Dan who was crumpled against the hood of his car. Lizzie strained to hear what was said, but Anna's father's soft voice was lost in the void between them. They watched as his dark shape guided Dan onto the passenger seat before taking the driver's seat. The engine started up again and the Rambler made its way home four blocks away.

"I am so sorry," Lizzie said after they had gone. "I don't know what's happened to him. He was like this on Sunday, wasn't he, Anna?"

A knowing looked passed between Anna and her mother before they turned and walked back into the house. Anna's already told them, Lizzie thought to herself. It will be all over town soon that her uncle is a drunk. She could feel the warmth of embarrassment starting at the base of her neck. She remembered when they were in grade 5 how all the kids teased her classmate Alfie because his father was often seen drinking in the nearly teetotal town.

Later, Lizzie learned he was an alcoholic, but that was irrelevant when you're 10 years old and your father passes out on a public bench near your school. Alfie rarely spoke and seemed to pull himself into the smallest space possible in an attempt to be invisible. The class bullies had been relentless until a new boy joined their year and they spent their attention on him instead. She had not thought about Alfie for years. His family moved quietly away during the summer before grade 6 began.

Lizzie took a breath and steeled herself as she went into the house. Anna offered her a glass of orange juice and they sat at the pine kitchen table sipping their drinks listening to the hum of the refrigerator while they waited for Anna's father to return. Lizzie wanted them to say Dan would be all right but they seemed unable to look at her. She wanted to ask them to keep it to themselves but couldn't find the words.

A sudden loud rap on a wooden frame startled their trance. Anna's mother vaulted out of her chair to answer the front door. Lizzie saw her father standing behind the screen.

"Lizzie, ready to go?" he asked before he saw her moving towards the door. "Got your things? Your mom's waiting in the car."

"Just be a moment," Lizzie said running back into the kitchen to get a magazine Anna had given her.

When she returned, Anna's father had arrived on the porch and the three parents were standing in a close circle. They stopped talking as Lizzie approached. Lizzie thought her dad looked angry and guessed Anna's parents had told him about Dan's drinking.

"Thanks for having Lizzie," her dad said pulling her towards the car, "....and the other. We'll see you at church."

Lizzie's mother smiled as they got into the car. "Have a good time?" she enquired, but the smile dropped as Lizzie slumped into a corner.

"Yeah, fine," Lizzie gave the standard response staring out the window at Anna's porch as the light went off.

Her father twisted the key in the lock and the engine charged into motion. "Wasn't fine," he contradicted. "Dan's been drinking again. Gonna be a real problem if he doesn't stop it."

"Like you said before," her mother replied, "your parents are going to have to deal with this. I can't think about anything other than Sam at the moment."

"Just hope they can..." her father's voice trailed off and Lizzie wondered if he knew how to deal with a drunk.

25 July 2018

The clink of the wine glasses resounded around the dining room.

"Happy late birthday," Richard smiled at Elizabeth.

"Perhaps better not at all than late!" she quipped back.

"That's gratitude for you," their neighbour Grace scolded. "I'd be really pleased if someone arranged a birthday surprise for me." She cocked her head at her husband, Bob, sitting on the opposite side of the table.

"Look at the grief you're causing me," he said to Richard while smiling at Grace.

"It'll be your turn next," Elizabeth said to Grace, "so we'll find out soon enough what he can do!"

"Great," Bob muttered, "that really helped."

The others burst out laughing and took a sip of wine. There was a snuffle on the baby monitor. Kiera paused and leaned toward the sound but relaxed when Zoe settled into a deeper sleep.

Dave held up the water jug. "Would you like some more?"

"I'd prefer what you're having," she mourned.

"It's the worst, isn't it?" Bob and Grace's daughter Louise said. "Just when you need it the most, you're not allowed to drink."

"Oh, don't rub it in," Kiera told her lifelong friend. "I'll be so glad when she's weaned."

"Wait until the two's," Louise warned as her husband Jack nodded in agreement. "You'll really need an occasional glass then!"

"Children must be getting worse," Elizabeth said to the other three members the older generation at her end of the table. "My parents coped perfectly well without drink at all."

"Yeah," chided Richard, "Look at how that's turned out."

Elizabeth slapped him playfully on the arm. "Have you got any more in that bottle or not?"

Richard re-filled her glass with white wine and collected up the dinner plates.

"It's the difference between country and city, isn't it?" Grace said.

Elizabeth looked at her blankly.

"The drinking…" Grace went on. "You and I grew up in the country, in the 60s! The most sophisticated thing we ever had to drink was Hawaiian Fruit Punch! You could zing it up with ginger ale if you really wanted a good time out." Grace laughed. "I think we even had a ring of lemon sorbet in it once. That was real sophistication!

"While us boys," Bob took over, "had the cultured environment of the city. Our parents did their networking at dinner parties with wine."

"And all the kids had a taste of something alcoholic on the sly before they were 15." Richard said as he came into the room carrying a cake.

"So some things stay the same, then," Jack smirked. "Louise had tried a lot more than I had when we met."

"And what about you, Kiera?" Dave asked. "I seem to remember stories of you getting into the cocktails a couple of times."

"That was only when *they*" Kiera nodded to the set of parents, "were making mojitos or sundowners."

"You make us sound like lushes!" Elizabeth laughed. "We did that once….and regretted it the next morning." A sudden memory of her father's disapproving grimace when Sam brought home a can of beer swept through her.

Occasionally, she was caught in surprise at the distance she had moved from her childhood – not just in miles but in the tenets of her life. The clockwork church attendance had dissolved into a possible holiday visit, an absolute abstinence had evolved into using wine as an enjoyable pastime and the strength of the core family unit was now stretched to a few emails a year with Christmas cards.

"You can blow out the candles," she heard Richard say. The past was brushed aside again as she focused on the celebration in front of her. The 6 and 5 shaped candles blew out with a slight puff. Richard handed her a large carving knife with a theatrical bow.

Elizabeth sliced through the thick moist layers of Devil's Food cake and loaded a piece onto a plate for each of them. She then ran a finger along the blade to collect the ganache that remained and sucked the finger clean of the chocolate icing.

"Yum, Kiera," she praised her daughter, "that is perfect."

"It's not easy when you're sleep deprived!" Kiera retorted. Just then a small cry from the monitor grew louder. Kiera eyed up her portion of cake and sighed. "She'll be hungry."

By the time Kiera returned with the drowsy infant in her arms, the others had moved into the sitting room and fresh glasses of wine had been poured and consumed. Kiera dropped Zoe into Dave's lap and followed her mother into the kitchen to help make coffee.

Elizabeth eyed the box of chocolates lying amongst discarded wrapping paper and ribbons. It wasn't a question of whether she wanted one, but whether she could share. Richard knew exactly where to find her favourite chocolates which were only sold in a tiny shop down town. With some reluctance, she decided to include them on the tray with the cafetiere filled with freshly ground coffee, cups and sugar and mentally applauded herself for being so magnanimous.

"Did you ever track down your pen pal?" Kiera asked unexpectedly as they waited for the water to boil.

"Wasn't sure he'd want me to," Elizabeth admitted.

"Even though you'd written for all those years?"

"There was just something in his last letter that seemed like goodbye." Elizabeth knew it sounded weak when she said it out loud.

"But don't you want to know what happened to him?" Kiera persisted. "Just out of curiosity? I know I would. I look up old classmates sometimes just to see if I can find out what's happened to them. There was one girl in high school – Molly – she was such a dizz, always late to class, but you know what? She's running her own company now! Really doing well! So hard to tell how people are going to end up."

"Maybe..." Elizabeth still hesitated.

"You remember Zac – my junior year? Boy did I have a thing for him. I thought we were going to be the best couple. Don't tell Dave, but I looked Zac up and, you know what? I really dodged a bullet there. He's an accountant for a shoe factory somewhere in Pennsylvania. Really sounded dull."

Elizabeth listened as her daughter recounted her own searches for former friends and wondered if she could trace Anna. The weekend back in Indiana had refreshed the longing for her childhood friend. She wondered if they would still be friends if Anna hadn't moved away. As Kiera pointed out, people change and there never were any guarantees. They had been so inseparable when they were young that Elizabeth could still feel the bonds that connected them. She wondered if that was just an illusion or a corrupted memory. JJ had said Anna moved to the south of the state, along the river and maybe, Elizabeth thought to herself, that was a place to start looking for her.

28 July 1968

The annual church picnic was held in the town's park, just a few blocks away from the church's central position. Lizzie and her family rushed home after the Sunday service to change out of their best clothes into something more casual and to fill their picnic basket with items from the oven and bowls of salads from the refrigerator. By the time they arrived at the park, the tables under the pavilion roof had already been lined up and covered from a huge roll of paper.

Lizzie's father carried the heavy picnic basket from the car. Johnny grabbed the large Thermos gallon jug filled with punch. Sam held a carrot cake while Lizzie took a deep dish apple pie.

They staked out their dining area with paper plates weighted down with cutlery and plastic tumblers. Barbara, Tom and the twins spread out their dinnerware opposite them along with Grandpa Ernest and Grandma Mary. Lizzie hovered near the edge of their place settings, holding space for Anna and her parents.

The foil covered dishes were set out down the middle of the long table, waiting for the blessing to be said. Lizzie loved this part of the picnic, when everything was being delivered and no one knew what anyone had brought. There were always standard items like the fried chicken and potato salad that someone always brought. But there were also family favourite casseroles and new experiments that made the dinner truly pot luck. It was tempting to try a sneaky finger in a dish but Lizzie knew she would get told off if she was caught.

The teenagers lounged on the hard benches while the meal was laid out. Younger children ran to the sets of swings and the roundabout where they punctuated the afternoon with their squeals and screams.

At last, the final families, including Anna and her parents, arrived and the minister called for them to bow their heads. After a prayer that Lizzie felt took longer than required, they were allowed to sample the riot of dishes that were passed down the long length of the table.

Anna eyed up Lizzie's plate that became piled high with a spoonful from each dish that circulated. Lizzie caught her looking and felt shamed.

"It's just a small taste of each one," she tried to explain. "Did you try the chicken casserole?"

Anna just shook her head.

"Here's some salad," Lizzie argued, pointing to a pile of lettuce that was amply covered in thousand island dressing.

"Wasn't me trying to lose weight," Anna said as she took a bite of her mother's meatloaf speciality. "What about you know who?" she added mischievously. "He could be coming any day now."

Guilt overtook Lizzie and she stared mournfully at the mound of food in front of her. Why, she thought, did it have to be so hard to give up eating?

Johnny reached across her to grab a bread roll and gave a wink at Anna. "Tried any more rowing since last week?" he asked her.

"Not a lot of chance for that," Anna laughed. "I'll need to get a boat first."

Anna's parents hunched over their plates, and gave short responses when Barbara asked them how they were. After a couple of attempts at starting a conversation with them, Barbara gave up and shrugged her shoulders lightly at Lizzie's mother.

Grandpa Ernest sat quietly while Grandma Mary chattered with another lady from the sewing group about how the quilts were coming along. Tom was telling a story about a customer he had visited during the week and getting a laugh when he told how the family dog had gotten into their car when it had been left idling and managed to knock the lever into drive and start off. Fortunately the damage was minor as the car gently crashed into a tree, he said, but it was bad news for the dog who still had to take his driving test.

"Clean up your plate, Lizzie," her mother scolded. "Everyone else is ready for desert."

Lizzie shoved a last painful amount into her mouth and chewed slowly. The casseroles and platters were cleared away and a new set of dishes was set out. Another train of food started around the table, enticing Lizzie with pies, cakes, cookies and an assortment of puddings. She caught Anna's glance of disapproval and restrained her choice to one piece of cherry pie. She noticed Anna took a piece of the carrot cake, two cookies and a dollop of chocolate pudding covered with whipped cream and felt virtuous by comparison.

When the plates were scraped clean and the covers put back on the remains of the desserts to keep out the flies, the young children ran, shouting, back to the play equipment and the adults stretched out to allow the food to seep into more comfortable corners of their stomachs.

The husbands and wives naturally drifted to opposite ends of the table, forming same sex clusters whose topics of conversation were gender driven. Lizzie's mother motioned for Mrs O'Neill to take the seat next to her.

"Ruth," she asked, "how are you? Have you had any news about Fred?

Ruth O'Neill shook her head, glancing down at the napkin she was twisting between her hands in her lap. "Nothing."

"Oh, how do you manage?" Lizzie's mother commiserated. "I'm so scared just thinking of Sam being called up."

Ruth raised her head.

"He got his draft notice this week," Lizzie's mother explained, a tremor in her voice. "He's got to go in on the 6th of August."

Ruth reached out a hand and covered her friend's hand. "It will be whatever the Lord allows."

"I think you're braver than me."

"It's not brave when you do the only thing you can do," Ruth replied. "That is, keep on living and hoping."

At the other end of the table, the men focussed on cars, farming and the batting averages of their favourite baseball players. Support for a professional baseball team was split with most of them backing either the Chicago White Sox or the Detroit Tigers, but one family had moved into town from Ohio and kept their allegiance to the Cleveland Indians.

The baseball talk inspired the male teenagers to haul out their catcher's mitts, a softball and bats from their family cars. Plastic picnic plates were appropriated for impromptu base markers over the protestations of Jerry Farr's mother that she didn't want them broken. Teams were assembled through selection by self-appointed team captains, Johnny and his friend Aiden, as they attempted to keep the teams evenly matched for skill, age and size.

The crack of the bat hitting the ball blended with the cheers of the players and the screaming from the playground to make the soundtrack of a summer's afternoon. Lizzie sat with the other girls in the shade of the pavilion, sipping tall glasses of punch from the Thermos jugs, too content to move.

Aiden's team went up to bat at the start of the 5th inning. They were leading by two runs and Johnny was shouting at his team to do better. Lizzie wondered if they would manage to play the full nine innings as she could feel restlessness beginning to build among the adults. The afternoon would end when the farming families had to leave to do evening chores.

Aiden came up to the home plate and took a couple of practice swings to loosen up. Jerry tossed the ball back and forth restlessly between his right hand and his gloved left hand and then drew himself up as he went for the throw. Aiden swung and missed.

"More like that," Johnny shouted encouragement from his position guarding first base.

Lizzie saw a glint of sunlight on metal flash behind the trees at the far side of the field as fast as a silverfish sliding back into darkness. Aiden whipped the bat hard and smashed against the ball. It flew high inside the first base line and he ran towards Johnny. Ray O'Neill was covering the outfield and followed the line of the ball with the line of his face. He ran back and back, face uplifted and focussed, his hand outstretched and ready to catch the fly ball, oblivious to the sounds around him. Suddenly, a car came charging around the curve of the road running alongside the park.

The picnickers heard a screech of brakes and the thwack of body on automobile. The car skewed to a stop. Ray disappeared behind a line of tall grass. Andrew O'Neill was the first to race across the grassy field toward the spot where he had last seen his son standing. Ruth O'Neill crumpled beside Lizzie's mother, gasping for breath and shaking.

Lizzie waited with the women and watched as the baseball players ran to the roadside to help. Johnny was the first to get there. It was then that Lizzie realised she knew the car. It was Dan's Rambler. She saw Anna recognised it as well and thoughts of the incident at

Anna's house on Thursday came flooding back. Lizzie breathed a prayer that he wasn't drunk this time and that Ray would be alright.

At a distance, all Lizzie could see was a group of people standing close together. The family living opposite the park flooded onto their porch to find out what had happened. There were shouts back and forth and suddenly Aiden was racing across to the pavilion.

"Dad," he panted, "they're getting an ambulance. Can you come and help."

The older man had just run from his car with the first aid kit that he always kept there. He was a volunteer fireman and trained for emergencies.

Ruth O'Neill caught Aiden's arm.

"Tell me," she begged.

Aiden looked scared. "He got caught under the wheel."

"Oh, Jesus, please," Mrs O'Neill moaned. Lizzie's mother supported the trembling woman on the walk to the site of the accident.

Lizzie stayed at the pavilion, not wanting to see the injuries or hear anything unpleasant. She had always been squeamish with any kind of injury. When one of the animals was hurt or taken to be butchered, she couldn't face the sight of blood. It had been even worse when Johnny had stepped on a nail once and had to be taken to the emergency room for treatment. She had refused to go anywhere near him for days until she was sure his foot had healed.

It wasn't long before Lizzie heard a siren. The ambulance service was provided by the fire department located just a few blocks away. The rising and falling wail of urgency only added to the anxiety Lizzie already felt. She rocked from one foot to the other as she stood watching the ambulance pull alongside the Rambler. The two men who got out disappeared behind the grass verge as they went to inspect the patient.

There was a long pause which, to Lizzie, felt endless. A second siren could be heard in the distance gaining volume as it neared. The sheriff's car drew up next to the other vehicles. A tall thin officer pulled his hat on as he got out of the car and started to inspect the Rambler. Lizzie could see a cluster of men form around him as they waved at the car and gestured towards the ground.

There was an exhale of breath as the paramedics stood up from behind the tall grass hefting a stretcher carrying Ray. They loaded it into the back of the ambulance and helped Mrs O'Neill climb in next to her son before the doors were shut, the siren re-started and the vehicle sped off to the hospital in Fenton

Lizzie turned to speak to Anna, but she had moved. Lizzie twisted around searching for her friend and saw she was walking with her parents to their car. Lizzie wondered why she hadn't said goodbye but then realised it was probably embarrassing for them to watch another encounter with her uncle. She knew she would prefer not to be there either.

The older men had remained in the pavilion. Lizzie saw the line of her grandfather's jaw harden as he stared at the offending vehicle and its driver. The officer opened the back door to his car and Dan got in. They sat talking in the car while the spectators waited to see what would happen. Milking time was approaching, but no one would leave until they knew how the culprit would be dealt with. At last, the engine started up and the sheriff's car drove away transporting Dan with it.

The family observing from the neighbouring house returned inside. The baseball players and their parents dispersed and wandered back to the pavilion.

Lizzie threw her mother a questioning glance as she neared the table.

"It's not good," her mother sighed deeply. "His leg's really bad and he may have broken an arm as well. They're not sure about internal damage."

She started packing away their plates and dishes into the picnic basket, clearing the paper rubbish to put into the bin. Looking down the table, she saw the debris of the O'Neill family's lunch and quietly started to clean and stack the plates to put away. Returning to the pavilion, Andrew O'Neill gruffly brushed her aside and clumsily dropped the plates into their basket. Lizzie's mother quietly handed him the dish with one remaining piece of cherry pie. He tossed it in with the plates and stomped awkwardly towards his car.

Johnny dragged all the baseball equipment back from the field. When he saw Mr. O'Neill leaving, he chased after him.

"Here," he called, "it's Ray's glove. He'll want…."

"NO," shouted Andrew O'Neill, "HE WON'T. Just take your baseball and your family and leave us ALONE." The car door slammed, stunning Johnny into silence. The engine revved and stones spat out as the gold Chevy spun out of the parking lot and onto the road.

Sam sat down beside his mother.

"Dad's gonna drive Dan's car back to theirs," He told her. He lowered his voice but Lizzie could still hear the disgust. "He was drunk, Mom. Again."

"Okay," her mother said, distracted. "We'll talk about it at home."

It wasn't until the milking and chores had been done and they were seated around the kitchen table again that conversation returned to what had happened.

"Ray's had surgery," Lizzie's mother told them. "Reverend Blake called your grandparents and said he would be alright, but it will take some time to get there. The leg was the worst. It was badly crushed and it's going to be hard to put it back together."

"I thought maybe Dan had killed him," Johnny whistled.

"Did he say anything to you, Dad, before they took him away?" Sam wanted to know.

Their father took a long drink of water before answering.

"I'm afraid he wasn't speaking very clearly."

"You mean he was drunk?" Johnny sneered.

"I'm afraid so," John Sr admitted. "Take this as a lesson in why to stay away from alcohol."

"I can't believe this happened," their mother said. "It's hard enough on all of them with Fred missing in action."

"He shouldn't be driving," Sam put in. "...at all! And it's the second time he's done it in a week."

Lizzie looked at her parents and realised no one had told her brothers about the incident on Thursday evening. It was worse than they knew. Anna and her parents knew more than they did and they could tell everyone in the church. Lizzie crossed her fingers and hoped they would keep it to themselves. She didn't want to be pitied or shunned for having an alcoholic in the family.

"How can we stop him?" Lizzie asked. "He is ruining everything."

"Don't worry," her father told her, "Grandpa will take care of this. He'll know what to do."

The conversation was finished and the matter closed, for now. They settled down as a family in the sitting room in front of the television because it was Sunday evening and time for the Ed Sullivan Show.

26 July 2018

Elizabeth remembered the day after her birthday surprise celebration why she didn't drink wine very often. Her father had called it alcohol's revenge. She struggled to lift her suddenly heavy head from the pillow. The aridness of a desert filled her mouth and she longed for water.

The other side of the bed was empty. She could hear distant voices and followed their sound to the kitchen where Richard was holding Zoe as Kiera made coffee.

"I was going to bring you a coffee in bed," Richard said, "after I had a quick hold of this one."

Elizabeth put a glass under the water faucet and let the cold water run over her hands. She lifted the glass carefully to her lips to combat a wave of nausea.

"Mom, you look awful," Kiera said brightly. "Guess having a baby is good for keeping away hangovers. Although I don't like the early morning starts."

"Why don't you sit down," Richard told his wife, " and I'll make up some breakfast?"

Elizabeth felt her stomach contract at the thought of food.

Dave appeared in the doorway, his hair still wet from the shower. He gently gathered up his daughter to free Richard for cooking.

Elizabeth nursed her coffee as Richard spun around the kitchen sliding bacon under the grill, breaking eggs onto a skillet and shoving bread into the toaster. Kiera pulled out plates and bowls and lined up boxes of cereal across the table.

Elizabeth picked through a spoonful of egg, moving it around the plate to appear that she had eaten something, but was not prepared to prompt her stomach into revolt. She looked suspiciously at her cheerful husband and wondered if her glass had been topped up more times than she remembered the night before.

She let Richard and Kiera lead the breakfast conversation. Their voices ebbed and flowed around her without much meaning. Dave drummed the table top with his fingers, anxious to be heading back now that the celebrations were finished: he had brought work home to compensate for being away overnight and needed time to complete it.

Finally, Kiera sighed and turned to her mother. "We'd better be off so Dave can bring home our bacon."

"Well," Dave said, "until your maternity leave is over, I *am* the sole breadwinner."

"So," Richard chided, "you're in charge of both bacon and bread, Dave?"

"That must make me in charge of eggs!" Kiera laughed. "Give me a minute and I'll get my hatchling ready to go." She scooped up Zoe for one last diaper change before their drive home.

Richard picked up his keys and a file of papers he had abandoned on the oak desk which had arrived from Indiana. There was a flurry of goodbyes and doors closing as the house emptied, leaving Elizabeth to contemplate the stacks of dirtied dishes left on the kitchen table. She poured the last tepid cup of coffee from the cafetiere and let the caffeine work through her bloodstream to counter the nausea.

A sliver of sunlight ran through the house and across the golden oak of her father's desk. She had spent the flight home mentally repositioning it around her house. In the end, they had placed it on the western side of the house, next to a window overlooking the back yard. The reading chair that sat in that position moved closer to the fireplace.

She would need to be determined if this desk was to remain only hers. Already she had seen its casual appropriation by Richard leaving his file here. It was too easy to use the horizontal surface to collect passing papers, ornaments or keys. She didn't want that. She ran a hand along the edge, breaking the beam of sunlight.

It had always been her father's private space. No one else had been allowed to delve into the desk drawers. It was the helm from which the farm was run. Every detail of every cow in the herd, every invoice for feed and vets, and every cheque stub and tax return had been stored here. Her father had struggled with computerisation and, in the end, gave up trying. The drawers had been bulging with scraps of history which they had taken out and discarded. And now the desk was hers.

Elizabeth dragged a kitchen chair over and settled into the central space of the desk. The haunting memory of her father sitting in this position jarred with the new outlook. It felt wrong to be looking at a suburban landscape and she wondered if she had been right to bring the desk here.

Throughout her life, the desk had been a centre for work but it was now in danger of being merely decorative. It needed a use.

Her laptop was sitting on the coffee table where she had left it yesterday after checking her emails.

Elizabeth placed it on the worn leather skiver embedded in the desktop. Pushing the power button on added a sense of purpose and she could feel invisible tendrils from the desk wrapping around the computer and fixing it into place.

As the remains of breakfast dried onto the morning's dishes, Elizabeth typed the name of her friend into Google for the second time: 159 million hits. It was even worse than when she had searched before. She reminded herself that it didn't really matter because Anna was probably married and had changed her name.

Elizabeth recalled JJ saying Anna had moved south to somewhere near the Ohio River. Maybe she could find out where she went to high school and start at a time when her name was still the same. She pulled up a map of Indiana and studied the names of the counties running along the river. The search was no longer just an idea but a project that needed a plan. Elizabeth rummaged through her kitchen drawers for a notebook and pen and then settled at the desk to list the counties in step 1.

She surprised herself with how little she knew about her home state. She suddenly realised how small her circumference of local knowledge was and that it didn't extend to the southern edge of the state. How could there be a county called Switzerland - which had a town called Warsaw? Were the early settlers so lacking in imagination that everything from Europe had to be recreated in this new country? She debated these questions as she listed the county names, excited that her quest was raising interesting details of history and geography that were independent of her search.

The next step took her to find the names of the high schools in each county. She set out a page for each county and noted down the names of every school. She was hoping that she might find Anna in Santa Claus, Indiana. But, maybe, that could only happen if she had been a good girl this year, she laughed to herself.

She sat back before launching into the next painstaking phase which would mean searching the old yearbooks and alumni records of the schools. The tightness in her head had eased but there was a growing hollowness from the lack of breakfast. Elizabeth poked through the refrigerator's contents and found some tuna mayonnaise to make a sandwich. She filled a glass with water and returned to her new work station.

The search consumed her afternoon. Each school website had its own unique layout and alumni sites that had to be examined. There were pages of photos to look at. Elizabeth methodically worked her way through the list, crossing off each entry when it failed to deliver a mention of Anna.

The drying crusts of the sandwich were left on the plate as she concentrated on the search. The sun shifted across the sky and started to edge its way through the picture window above the desk. Elizabeth tilted the screen away from the glare. She was about to close the laptop and stop for the day when she heard a key in the door. Richard looked surprised to see her sitting at the desk and then puzzled when he looked beyond her to the breakfast remains still laying where he had left them.

"You're back early," Elizabeth said.

"Not really." A slight accusatory tone slipped into his voice. "Bit late is more like it."

"Sorry," Elizabeth apologised. "I was just packing up." She moved to close the browser when an image on the screen caught her attention. She held her breath as she looked through the names at the side of the class photos.

"It's Anna!" She screamed.

"Your school friend?"

"I've been working on this all day. Now I know where she went to school."

"What?" Richard was surprised. "It's taken all day? Can't you just look her up on Facebook or something?"

"One," Elizabeth refused to be deflated, "she has a common name. "Two, I don't know if she changed it by getting married. Three, I don't want to announce my search – what if she doesn't want to know? Hard to be discreet if you plaster it all over Facebook."

"So, what's the next step?" Richard asked looking at the kitchen. "….hopefully after supper?"

"People would think you never ate," Elizabeth replied following his gaze. "Now I know where she was, I can look up her parents, check if she got married in the county, do a genealogy search." She glowed anticipating the hunt.

4 August 1968

It was the first time Lizzie ever remembered being anxious about going to church. She was desperate to see Anna. They had only spoken briefly during the week and then it was with Lizzie's mother nearby so she hadn't felt able to say too much. Anna said she was too busy to see her, but she didn't tell her what she was doing.

Lizzie had spent the week caught in the long cycle of food preservation. Along with more beans, they had moved on to making tomato juice and ketchup for the winter. The first flush of corn had started as well and Grandma Mary spent a day with them brushing the silk off the long cobs before they were blanched and the kernels cut off with sharp knives. Lizzie preferred cleaning corn to cutting it off. She accidentally sliced the side of her thumb once and knew the risks.

Lizzie asked her grandmother about Dan. The older woman shifted in her seat before answering slowly.

"He was wrong to be driving, Lizzie," she said. "Let it be a lesson. Alcohol causes so many problems in the world. We didn't raise him to drink and now look what's happened. That poor boy may never walk properly again."

She signalled the end of the conversation, but later, when Lizzie was returning to the kitchen from the bathroom, she overheard her mother and grandma speaking softly. Dan was charged with being drunk while driving and his parents would make sure he pleaded guilty.

Her dad and brothers moved on to chopping the green field corn to feed the silo. It would ferment into a smelly, slippery food that the cows loved during the winter. There was no mention of meetings in town or trips to the drive-in for ice cream. Even Sam stayed home instead of going out with Glenda.

After a week of seclusion, when Sunday came around Lizzie was eager to see Anna but nervous to see the rest of the congregation after the incident at the picnic. She shuffled the small selection of hangers with her Sunday best clothes trying to work out what to wear. Usually, she wore the first dress she put her hand on, but today felt different and deserving caution. Finally she chose a lime green A line dress with a hemline that hit just above the knee.

She wished she could wear trousers to church instead, but girls and women always wore dresses. At least she had the one pair of pantyhose to wear instead of a garter belt and stockings which led to awkward tugging on the fashionable short skirts when sitting to prevent unwanted exposure of bare skin on the upper thigh. Mini skirts were 'in' and while she longed for the figure to wear them, Lizzie prudishly thought they weren't appropriate for church. Sitting opposite a girl in a mini skirt was a gift to a hormone fuelled teenage boy, who could be rewarded with glimpses of forbidden flesh.

They got to church just as everyone was sitting down for Sunday school lessons. The teenagers met in the basement, gathered in a circle of folding metal chairs with Doris Feldman as the teacher. Johnny sat next to Lizzie, opposite Anna. Lizzie smiled at her friend who shrugged a reply. Anna slyly shifted her skirt when she saw Johnny drop his gaze to her legs, and became more agitated until Lizzie nudged Johnny to look up. A faint flush started at his collar and worked upwards when he realised he had been caught eyeing up a girl.

The boys in the group scoffed at the expected points of the lesson on the childless Abraham who God promised would become a father of nations despite being 99 years old. They smirked when told Abraham did not trust God to deliver and got a maid pregnant before he then had a son with his wife. Lizzie felt the object of the lesson - to trust in the Lord - had been lost on them as they focused on the more illicit details.

When the class came to an end, the group crammed the stairwell to join their parents in the sanctuary above. Anna was pulled along with the crowd before Lizzie could catch up to say hello but signalled she would see Anna later.

Johnny prodded Lizzie from behind as they came to the door of the sanctuary. Grandpa Ernest and Grandma Mary sat in their usual places in the front row, but the spaces around them remained empty as if an invisible wall was keeping people away. Lizzie's father stood at the back of room and signalled for them to sit with their grandparents. Grandma Mary gave a nervous smile as Lizzie and Johnny entered the empty row behind them but Grandpa Ernest sat straight, his gaze fixed forward.

The two rows filled as Sam and their mother settled beside Lizzie and Barbara and Tom filed in with the twins next to Grandma Mary. Lizzie's skin prickled with tension. She felt the weight of the stares from the congregation on her back and moved her head slightly to try and see where Anna was sitting out of the corner of her eye. Instead she caught the hard glare of Andrew O'Neill just as Lizzie's father slid in next to her and blocked the line of sight.

Crashing chords boomed from the pipe organ and the congregation stood for the first hymn. Afterwards, Lizzie couldn't remember exactly what the minister said in his sermon. When he said it was about the prodigal son, she watched her grandfather's jaw twitch and wondered if the topic was aimed at her family. The story of the profligate son met with nods along the pews but when the tale turned to the young man's return to his family, the heads locked into a stiff anger.

Lizzie was relieved when the interminable hour ended and the congregation filed out as the organist played the classical pieces he had practised during the week. They poured onto the sidewalk to exchange the week's news with friends, but found the sea of bodies swept away from their family. Lizzie tried to speak to Anna, but backs turned towards her as she approached.

Her mother called her to the car and they made a silent journey home. Grandpa Ernest and Grandma Mary were already there when they drove up the lane. They were usually some of the last to leave the church, as Grandpa Ernest stood talking to lifelong friends until eventually Grandma Mary would tug on his sleeve and pull him away because dinner was going to be spoiled.

Lizzie started laying the table as her mother flew around the kitchen turning on the heat under pans of vegetables and pulling the roast out of the oven to rest. Her brothers disappeared to change back into jeans and check shirts. Grandma Mary began filling the glasses with water to set on the table.

"It won't go away," Lizzie heard her father say.

"Nope," her grandfather agreed. "Their boy's not going to be out of hospital for some time. Can't forget that."

"Can't say I blame them either."

"Too much for one family. Their missing Fred, and Ray -- not knowing what will happen."

"Heard they can't afford it either." Lizzie's dad rubbed his hand along the back of his head. "Hospital's gonna cost. What if they sue?"

"Dan ain't got that kind of money. Can't even afford a lawyer, let alone pay for a hospital. Can barely pay for the new baby."

The two men stared out over the surrounding fields.

"Damn Dan." Lizzie had never heard her grandfather swear before.

"He's gone too far now. There won't be any fatted calf at my home," said Grandpa Ernest dismissing the sermon they heard only an hour before.

Sam and Johnny thundered down the stairs and spilled into the room. Lizzie took the diversion to slip away and change her own clothes. Everyone was sitting at the table when she returned. Grandpa Ernest led the blessing as they bowed their heads for the Sunday dining ritual. No blessing was asked for Uncle Dan.

28 July 1968

Delhi. I can't believe we are here in India! This is the first stop on our way to London. This is even noisier than Singapore. There's so much to see and no room on this card. Henry

28 July 2018

Elizabeth turned the postcard over in her hands. It was a standard tourist photo of the Red Fort in Delhi. She reached into the box and pulled out three more postcards which tracked Henry's journey across the world to London. The second leg took him to Istanbul and the postcard showed a traditional souk. From there the family flew to Berlin and another card had arrived showing the Brandenburg Gate. The card from their final destination pictured Buckingham Palace.

The messages grew more fevered as the trip progressed. She wondered how he had managed to buy cards and stamps on brief layovers between flights. Over her own years of travelling, she had gradually given up sending postcards to anyone. She hated spending time from her holiday writing platitudes about the wonderful time she was having just to show she had been somewhere. She had certainly never sent cards mid-journey.

The gift of this kindness suddenly overwhelmed her. Her finger stroked the softened edge of the English card. It had taken her 50 years to realise this was special and she felt ashamed for having taken it for granted. Maybe, she thought to herself, there had been more than just being pen pals.

She spread the cards out over the oak desk. She had intended to continue her search for Anna, but now felt drawn to look for Henry once again—just to see what had become of him. She poked her laptop on and trawled through her mind to remember what Sam had said about English lawyers.

They were called solicitors, she recalled. She added 'English Solicitor' to Henry's name in a Google search and pressed the button. Suddenly, the top entry showed the name of a law firm in Leeds where he had worked until retiring 6 months before. There was no longer a photo of him among the staff, but Elizabeth felt certain this must be her Henry. It was too much of a coincidence.

Elizabeth was a reluctant user of social media. Her Facebook account was mainly to keep in contact with Kiera and for occasional updates from Sam or Johnny. She only allowed access to her family and a few close friends. The thought that a stranger could access her photos worried her constantly. Being retired, she considered the connections of LinkedIn unnecessary, but she realised many professional people would use it and Henry could be listed on it.

The thought of finding his profile tempted her. She would need to set up her own profile to use the system but then she wondered what would be the point. Richard had told her that if you look at someone's profile, they could see who had viewed it. She didn't know if she was ready to be discovered. Elizabeth stretched and got up from the chair. She flicked on her new electric kettle and listened as it rumbled into a boil.

The sound took her back to when she first saw an electric kettle in Henry's house. The English were fascinated with their tea. No discussion could start without a brew having been made and cups being poured. Even when she had landed on his doorstep without notice, the awkward moment was swept aside by pulling out the teapot. She discovered that in the 1970s while Americans revelled in more household appliances than much of the rest of the world, the English could boil water faster with their electric kettles.

It was during her student year in Paris while studying for her French degree that she made the journey to Leeds. Her friend had pushed her into making that trip. Helen was her roommate in an impossibly old fashioned boarding house set in the 5th Arrondissement near the universities of the Sorbonne. By spring and the Easter break, they had had their fill of roaming the narrow streets of the Left Bank, sitting in the cafes and browsing through the books shops in their free time.

Elizabeth told Helen about the years of sporadic correspondence with Henry which had become more infrequent when they moved on to university. Her friend pointed out as she was on the same side of the Atlantic Ocean, this might could be her one chance to meet him face to face. Armed only with his last known address and backpacks of clothes, they set out on an adventure to Leeds.

The ferry across the channel had eaten a sizeable portion of their meagre budget, so when they landed on English soil they stuck out their thumbs for a free ride. It had been an adventure that Elizabeth never admitted to her daughter. Today there were very few hitchhikers to be seen on the roads, but in 1973, the laybys on the motorways were lined with hopefuls holding signs for their destinations.

When they arrived at Henry's door, they had spent 18 hours negotiating the roads of England northward from Dover with only a damp map and an address to guide them. They were grey with dirt and tired after a night sheltering in a motorway café.

Suddenly, when faced, finally, with meeting Henry, Elizabeth had hesitated. It was Helen who boldly rapped on the door. With only a flicker of surprise, Henry gave his widest smile and welcomed them in. Elizabeth still remembered the overwhelming ease of their arrival and being coddled in acceptance. Something inside her felt connected.

Henry was as exotic as the blurry photos had suggested. His long dark hair fell below his shoulders and was held in place with a beaded headband across his forehead. He had smouldering intense eyes that always seemed to ask a question. His faded jeans and paisley shirt matched the bohemian look and Elizabeth had been grateful their first meeting had been there and not on her parents' farm.

His parents were absent on holiday and only Henry and his sister Susan were home. Friends from university arrived on news of the visitors and the night disappeared in a blur of coffee, music and talk.

Elizabeth still remembered it as the most unexpected night of her life.

She spooned out instant coffee into a cup while she waited for the water to boil. A goldfinch hopped onto the bird table, challenging a sparrow for the seeds. The kettle's churning peaked and Elizabeth poured the hot water over the granules and added milk. She cupped the mug in both hands and sipped slowly while watching the birds squabble over food. Finally, the sparrow flew away and she made a decision.

Back at the keyboard, she opened up the LinkedIn website and keyed in her personal information. She kept the profile as sparse as possible and deliberately declined to add a photo. Finally, she could search and within moments she found his page. The photo looked like the professional headshot that would have been on his firm's website. His face had lost its sharp angles and he had broadened away from the teenage lankiness she remembered. He didn't look 65 though. She thought the photo might be 15 to 20 years old.

Henry's profile was as lean as her own. They seemed to share a reticence to reveal too much which now felt ironic after spending so many hours when they were young reciting their limited lives.

There was an invitation to make contact on the webpage, to send a 'like' or a message. Her hand hovered over the keys ready to crash into his life once again. Instead, she closed down the browser and folded the laptop lid. She wasn't ready to face another collision of their worlds.

6 August 1968

The alarm was set for 5 am. Her dad and brothers were used to that early hour, getting up in the dark for another round of milking and feeding, but normally Lizzie didn't make it out of bed before 7.30. It had been hard to get to sleep and then she woke up several times. Her mind felt as restless as her body and refused to settle.

Sam wasn't helping with chores today. Instead he would load his duffel bag into the car and their mother would drive him into Fenton so he could get the bus to the induction centre. Lizzie couldn't believe he might not come back. Her stomach twisted when she thought of him being sent to some jungle in Vietnam or learning how to kill. He never even joined the hunters in the autumn or fired a gun. A war that was so far away had suddenly become touchingly close.

Lizzie's mother's red rimmed eyes countered the measured sentences she spoke.

"Tell him, goodbye, Lizzie," she said. "We'll need to be off."

Sam reached out to her in a gawky unfamiliar hug and she let him pull her to him for a brief moment. Johnny playfully punched him on the shoulder and wished him well.

Their dad stood tall and held out a large calloused hand to shake. He swallowed Sam's hand in his and covered it with his other hand, reluctant to release the hold and let his son disappear. Finally, he pulled away and let the hand drop.

"Be safe, son," he said. "Come back."

They stood and watched as the tail lights of the car shrank with distance. At last, Lizzie's father turned towards the barn and the sound of baying cows.

Lizzie slid through the dew covered grass and sat down on the step to the front door. She wrapped herself in the pre-dawn darkness and listened as the pumps of the milking machine started up. The sky gradually lightened the landscape into greys of mist and shadow before spreading pale washes of colour. A hot line of yellow and orange blazed on the horizon before the sun edged across. The rising sun cast long shadows across the lawn. More cars moved along the road as another day began.

At last Lizzie heard the sound of their car crunching gravel along the lane. She stretched out her legs and rubbed warmth into her arms before rising to meet her mother.

"Been there all this time?" her mother queried.

Lizzie nodded.

"Come on, help me with breakfast," her mother said. "It'll be alright. I'm sure of it." She tried to sound hopeful, but Lizzie heard the quaver in her voice.

The meal felt awkward. Even though they got used to eating with just the four of them while Sam was away at college, the absence now was disturbing. They pushed pancake pieces around their plates and tried to talk over the music playing on the radio.

The news came on and the newsreader talked about the Republican Convention that had started the day before. Lizzie sighed. It would be three more nights without her favourite TV shows. The Conventions took over all three channels as if nothing else was important. She loved watching The Beverley Hillbillies, even if it was a summer repeat.

Lizzie spent the morning helping her mother clean house, pulling out cabinets to sweep behind them and needlessly running a cloth over ornaments that were already free of dust. Whenever she tried to sit, her mother found another job for her to do until it was time for lunch.

Her father and Johnny had been working in a field along the road and stopped to collect the mail when they came back up the lane. Johnny had his teasing smile on when they came through the door and he hefted the roll of mail onto the kitchen counter. He pulled out a colourful piece of card and brandished it at her.

"What's this then?" he mocked.

"Haven't a clue what you're on about," Lizzie told him.

"It's a postcard from Delhi. India. For you," he accused as if it were a crime.

"Well, let me see it then." Lizzie made a grab for the postcard which Johnny held high over her head.

"Johnny," her mother scolded, "hand it over. It's not yours."

Lizzie stared at the alien scene on the card. The red buildings were unlike any she'd ever seen before. When she started writing to Henry, she had looked in their set of encyclopaedias to find out more about Singapore. The pictures were in black and white and showed urban scenes with a few skyscrapers and water fronts lined with boats. None of that was familiar to Lizzie but this coloured image of the fort seemed even more remote from the buildings she was used to seeing. There were small figures dressed in saris and Lizzie thought she could feel the heat of the Indian sun.

She turned the card over as Johnny tried to peer over her shoulder to see what it said.

"Who's Henry?" Johnny asked. "That your boyfriend?"

"Just a *friend*." Lizzie pulled the card into her body so he couldn't see it. "Just forget about it," she told him, knowing that he would. He'd already forgotten that she had a pen pal even though the letters had been coming for a couple of years.

"Why's he in India?" Johnny persisted.

"'Cause he's moving to England," Lizzie told him and then, under her breath, said, "which means he won't be coming here." She floated between relief and loss. Maybe, she told herself, it was better that he didn't come. How likely had it been anyway that his whole family would travel to Indiana on a journey around the world? She could see that hope had given more substance to the idea than it deserved. But as much as she was scared at the prospect of meeting Henry, she mourned the lost opportunity. And only Anna would understand.

"I don't think I'd like India," Johnny said as he took his seat at the table while Lizzie stowed the postcard in a drawer to retrieve later.

After lunch and Lizzie had wiped dry the dishes her mother washed, she was released from chores for the afternoon. Lizzie immediately jumped on her bicycle and headed down the rutted road into town. She passed Harrison's Home Stores and counted the three street crossings before turning left into Anna's road.

She thumped on her friend's door and then stood back embarrassed that she had knocked so loudly. Anna opened the door cautiously but relaxed when she saw Lizzie.

"Sorry," Lizzie said. "Didn't mean to bang so hard."

"Guess there aren't any dents."

"Said sorry."

"Don't worry," Anna said. "Not gonna be our door for much longer anyway."

"What?" Lizzie was confused.

"Needed to tell you," Anna added, moving to the swing bench seat. "We're moving. Dad's got a new job and, well, we have to go...." Her voice trailed off in uncertainty.

"No," Lizzie cried. "When? You can't go. You never told me." The fear tumbled out in a tangle of words.

"I know it's a shock." Anna spoke with a stillness in her voice. "It's got to be soon so I can get settled into a new school."

"I can't lose you as well," Lizzie moaned.
"As well as?"

"Everyone," Lizzie sighed. "No, it's Sam. He went for induction this morning. And then, well, Henry's not coming either."

"Well, you don't have to worry about the doughnuts now," Anna teased.

"I know." Lizzie looked out across the street at a view she had seen many times before. "Part of me is relieved, I have to admit, but then I wonder if I will ever meet him. England is a long way away."

They held a moment's silence in mourning of the lost opportunity, rocking the swing bench gently using their feet.

Lizzie turned to Anna. "Why didn't you tell me you were moving?"

"It came up really fast. My dad just had this offer he couldn't refuse," Anna explained. "Didn't know until last week if he was going to take it."

"How soon?"

"Next week." Anna replied. "We're already starting to box everything up. Such a big job – it's all my mom and I are doing now. Never moved before. You suddenly realise how much junk you've got! I've got teddies from when I was a baby!"

Lizzie half listened while Anna chattered about the things she had found in her room. She felt dazed by the tornado of change that was spinning around her. She was certainly dizzy and the ground seemed to tilt suddenly.

"Are you all right?" Lizzie heard Anna from a distance. "You don't look too good."

Lizzie heard the screen door bang and voices. A cold wet glass was pushed into her hand.

"Here, have a drink of water," Anna's mother said.

Lizzie sipped the water and slowly felt the ground level and a warmth come back into her face.

"Sorry," she said. "Don't know what happened."

"Didn't think you'd miss me THAT much," Anna tried to joke but Lizzie couldn't smile.

"Just took you by surprise," Anna's mother said pragmatically. "Kind of felt like that for us as well."

"I never thought of you leaving," Lizzie said to her friend.

"Yeah," Anna replied sadly. "Me neither, but as they say, 'The Times, They are a Changing'".

"Guess so," Lizzie begrudged. "I always thought we'd finish school together."

"What can I say? Things don't always turn out the way you think." Anna looked glum. "I'm definitely feeling that."

They rocked on the bench watching the occasional car pass while Anna's mother went back inside to continue packing. The day seemed ordinary enough to Lizzie. There was no sign that anything exciting was happening and yet, she thought to herself, everything had changed since yesterday.

Anna did most of the talking, explaining how they had to get her school reports sent to her new school and her parents had been trying to find a house for them. With that and the packing, there hadn't been much time.

Finally, Lizzie said she needed to head home. Anna's mother offered to drive her and Lizzie was grateful after her dizzy spell not to have to pedal the bicycle. It was left, leaning against the corner of the house, to be picked up later.

Sitting in the back seat, Lizzie watched the passing farms.

"What's the new job like?" she asked out of politeness.

"Oh," Anna's mother said looking across at her daughter beside her in the front seat, "it's similar, but with better pay. And we'll have big expenses coming up."

"Yeah, I suppose," Lizzie agreed. "I haven't thought about college yet. Guess it costs a lot. Don't know how Mom and Dad do it with both Sam and Johnny now at college." Her voice trailed off as she remembered Sam may not be going back to college this year.

Lizzie's mother was picking tomatoes in the garden when they drove in. She was surprised to see Lizzie emerge from the car.

"Where's the bike?" she said walking up to the car.

"She went a bit dizzy," Anna's mother replied. "We were worried about her riding back."

"You all right?"

"Just a bit of shock, I guess," Lizzie explained as she nodded towards Anna. "They're moving away next week."

Her mother looked up sharply at Anna's mother. "Really? So soon?"

"Well, we've got to get school and the house sorted before September. So, the sooner, the better."

Lizzie's mother nodded. "Guess that makes sense. Sorry you've got to go

"I'm sorry too," Anna said before getting back into the car.

Her mother wrapped an arm around Lizzie's shoulders as they stood watching the car disappear down the road.

1 August 2018

The small vegetable patch was becoming overrun. Elizabeth grimaced as she tried to clear the area around the tomato plants. She had never enjoyed weeding. She could admit she wasn't a very good gardener and often wondered why she tried year after year to coax uncooperative plants to provide produce for their dining table. It must be a remnant defective gardening gene, she said to herself, that wouldn't release her from the hope of better crops in the future.

Every spring she tackled the tangled remains of the small square, digging and pulling until the ground was ready for sowing. The conservatory was lined with plastic pots scattered with seedlings cajoled into life by the warmth of the house. There was always so much expectation at that time of year before the plants were set out and the first round of disease swept through the garden.

Elizabeth picked off three ripening tomatoes to catch them before they were eaten by the insects who gouged out their fleshy hearts leaving only a shell behind. She stood up straight, taking in the neighbouring yards. Theirs was the only vegetable patch in sight. Just like her, she thought, keeping a reminder of the vanishing life she had left which stood her apart from the life she had moved into.

When she opened the door to the kitchen she was met with voices from the Public Radio station. Elizabeth set the bowl of tomatoes on the counter and turned the kitchen radio to a golden oldies station. She was tired of the constant debate on NPR about whether President Trump had tried to obstruct justice or if there had been Russian interference in the election. The arguments swirled around constantly but none of them seemed capable of ending.

"Someone left the cake out in the rain" she sang with the radio as she pulled out the vegetable drawer and picked through the wilted remains of last week's shopping. The end of the cucumber, as always, was dissolving into a slippery ooze. They never seemed to be able to finish a whole one before decay set in.

She filled the sink with soapy water and began sponging the plastic box to rid it of residual mould. She wiped down the drawer, nestled the tomatoes in one corner and slid it back into the refrigerator. As she turned to wipe her hands dry, she glimpsed the dishevelled stack of papers on the desk.

Elizabeth sank with a heavy drop into the chair and picked up the top sheet. Her squiggles of French were strewn across the page roughly following the first two lines of "I wandered lonely as a cloud" by Wordsworth. She had always wanted to see how you could move between languages with poetry. She spent her working life exchanging words from one language with another but had never attempted translating poetry. She felt it was the ultimate challenge to maintain the rhythm and character of a poem with different words. So far success had eluded her.

'Are you going to Scarborough Fair, parsley, sage, rosemary and thyme.' The radio had changed to Simon and Garfunkel.

Suddenly in her mind Elizabeth saw the layby where she and Helen had waited for five hours to get a lift on their way to Leeds. They held out weary thumbs but got splashed as cars raced by their sliver of tarmac without stopping. There had been a sign to Scarborough. They didn't know where that was but they knew the song and sang it on a loop while jumping to keep warm. Finally, a truck driver stopped and they climbed up into his welcoming high cab.

In a moment's curiosity, she centred the laptop on the desk, lifted the lid and keyed in 'Scarborough, England'. Maybe she could finally see where it is after all this time. The city map filled the screen. The town sat at the edge of the land overlooking the sea. She zoomed out on the image to see where it sat within the country and there was Leeds. She sat back hard in the chair staring at the confluence of roads that made the city. Somewhere in that maze was an alternative destiny she could have had.

"Are you working on that poem, again?" There was a rustle of papers as Richard peered out from the day's Washington Post.

"Not really. I can't get the scan right," she said still looking at the computer screen.

Richard pulled himself out of the chair and peered over her shoulder at the map.

"Going somewhere?"

"Already been!" she answered. "That song on the radio reminded me of something. Got near to Scarborough once."

"What, England? When was that – we didn't go near Scarborough when we went to London three years ago."

"Back when I was a student in Paris," Elizabeth explained. "Helen and I hitchhiked over during the Easter break."

"But you said you hadn't been to London before!"

"We kind of missed it and went around."

"Why?" Richard was confused. "There's so much to see."

"We were students," Elizabeth conjured, "and didn't have much cash. London was just too expensive." She didn't understand why she was holding back.

"How are you getting on with finding Anna?" Richard headed to the kitchen and she heard the refrigerator door being opened.

"Really good." Elizabeth pulled up the document where she stored the results of her searches. "Can you believe it -- I've found her marriage license! Now I can start looking to see if she's using the married name 'Myers'."

Richard returned carrying a glass of orange juice and settled back to finish the newspaper.

Elizabeth restlessly gathered up her stack of papers and went to put them into the middle desk drawer on the left. There was a small rattling as she opened it. She swept the space with her hand looking for the loose object.

"Ouch!" Elizabeth pulled out her hand to reveal a pinprick of blood on her finger. More cautiously, she gently tapped around inside and pulled out two metal campaign pins before bursting with laughter.

"What's up?" Richard looked up.

Elizabeth held up the pins. "You definitely couldn't use these for an election campaign now." One said 'Nixon is the One' and the other 'You Can't Lick our Dick'.

"I definitely don't want that second one," Richard said and smiled with mischief. "I like a good licking!"

"Maybe I should wear it – to keep others away!" Elizabeth retorted. "Funny how different things look 50 years on."

"Yeah, they didn't know he'd get impeached."

"Wonder what they'll say in 2068 about us and our president."

"Another unique legacy." Richard disappeared back behind the newspaper.

Elizabeth dropped the papers into the open drawer and slid it shut. She fingered the pins idly remembering it had been during the Republican convention that Anna said she was moving. She had come back from Anna's and that night they sat and watched the delegates parade around the convention floor carrying their banners for different candidates. Nixon had been the clear favourite at the convention and in her family. The conservative heart of Indiana wanted the man who promised to bring the Vietnam war to an end.

A notification pinged up on the screen – a brief email from Sam.

"E, the auctioneer has set a date for the sale," she read. "He thought it would do well on Labour Day with people being off work for the weekend. Will you be coming for it? Talk later, Sam."

She thumbed to the next month in the calendar and wrote SALE across the 3rd of September in big letters. She wasn't going to miss the last day the farm would be part of her life.

8 August 1968

Lizzie spent the afternoon laying on a recliner in the shade of the walnut tree reading the last chapters of *Airport* by Arthur Hailey. Anna recommended it after it hit the best sellers' list. The wintry setting of the book was a cool antidote to the hot day. She wanted to finish because the bookmobile was due tomorrow, but kept being distracted by the sound of a passing truck or an insistent fly. Through a gap in the branches she could see the line of a contrail forming high in the blue sky. The plane was probably headed to Chicago, she thought with the images of the fictional Lincoln International Airport from the book still in her mind.

She'd seen airports on the TV but she had never been to one herself.   Just something else to add to her list of 'things to do'. Travel was on that list. She wanted to see what other places were like.   When she started learning French, she didn't know why she was bothering, but discovered she liked the language and wanted to see where it was spoken.

Cousins on her mother's side of the family went to Quebec about three years ago and told her how everyone spoke in French.   Chris and Fred were at college and thought the city life there was 'tres chic'. They had talked about the trip nonstop at a family reunion later that summer and said she should go there despite a bombing campaign from separatist groups.

Lizzie leaned her head back and let the book droop into her lap. The heat felt heavy and she struggled to keep her eyes open. They had been up late the night before watching the Republican Convention from Miami Beach. She hadn't meant to watch, but there was nothing else on the TV. The family sat with glasses of Coca Cola and ice and waited for the delegates from Indiana to rise and parade around the conference hall.

It was strangely compelling to see blocks of delegates from each state wave their placards and march up and down the aisles in their straw hats and sashes. Each group became a tidal wave of colour and energy before they were called to cast their votes for the presidential nominees.

There was little doubt that Richard Nixon would be chosen as the candidate for the party, but, despite that, they waited for the delivery of the count from each state and measured it against the number Nixon needed to clinch the nomination.   They cheered when the Indiana delegates rose from their seats and filed into the aisles to take their lap of revelry. Johnny grappled through the coats in the closet and found the flags stapled to sticks that they carried for the Memorial Day parade. He passed them out and they stood waving their patriotism until the delegates sat back down.

It wasn't long after that before her father's chin was digging into his chest and they heard his heavy, slow breathing. The early mornings always took their toll at night. They were down to Minnesota's delegates when he had roused himself and staggered off to bed after confirming that Nixon was on target to win. Lizzie hadn't got to bed until nearly 1 am.

It was the crunch of tires on the gravel that made her prise her eyes open. Grandma Mary was behind the wheel of their four year old Cadillac. She stopped at the widening of the lane next to the house that served as a parking area.

"You sleeping or reading?" she asked as she closed the car door behind her.

"Bit of both," Lizzie admitted. "Trying to finish this before tomorrow."

"Well," her grandmother said generously, " you carry on and I'll help your mother get supper ready, then."

Lizzie wasn't going to argue with a chance to avoid kitchen duties. She pulled herself upright and tried again to focus on the book to finish the remaining fifty pages.

After less than five pages, she heard the chug of a tractor coming nearer and looked up in time to wave as Grandpa Ernest drove past. He shouted instructions at Johnny as they hitched up the bailer and flat wagon and headed to the field for one more round of baling. The soft thump of the pump started up as her father began the evening round of milking.

She felt the guilt of indolence and tried instead to concentrate on the words swimming across the pages. A soft breeze attempted to lift the soporific heat, but Lizzie's consciousness melted as her eyelids sagged shut. The book slipped down into her lap.

She was woken by the tractor returning to the barn, the wagon piled high with bales of hay. Lizzie rubbed her eyes and forced the chair into the upright position. She flicked through the pages and slid in a bookmark when she found the page she last remembered reading.

The grass was soft under her bare feet, but she grimaced when she trod on a stone on the path. The porch's screen door creaked as she pulled it open and the hum of conversation between her mother and grandmother as they worked in the kitchen paused.

"Finish your book?" her mother called.

"Not quite," Lizzie answered as the aroma of apple pie wafted over her.

"You'd better get it done. I can drop you in for the bookmobile tomorrow and then you can pick up your bike."

"Yeah, okay," Lizzie said heading to the bathroom to wash her hands.

"She left it at Anna's," her mother explained. "But, we need to make sure we get it back before they move next week."

"You didn't say it was so soon." Grandma Mary sounded annoyed by the news. Lizzie smiled to herself. For once, her mother was ahead of her grandmother on the latest gossip. But the corners of her mouth slid back down as she thought of the emptying house and the remaining two years of high school without her friend.

When she returned to the kitchen the discussion had moved on to the patchwork the church ladies were piecing together. Lizzie let it flow around her as she counted out seven plates to set out on the table. The kitchen door slammed as Johnny stomped his way through to the bathroom.

"Help yourself to towels if you want to take a shower and change," her mother called out to Grandpa Ernest as he followed through the door. "Plenty of time before supper."

Lizzie carefully laid out the plates and cutlery and filled the glasses with water for each setting. Just as she was finishing, her mother came into the dining room.

"Why so many plates?" she asked.

Lizzie stared at the table wondering what was wrong. They were always seven and then she remembered: Sam wasn't there.

"Guess I wasn't thinking," Lizzie shrugged. She gathered up the spare place setting and spread the others evenly around the table but couldn't fill the vacancy they felt.

"I know." Her mother's voice had a slight tremor. "I wish he would call."

When her father came in, they started to plate up the food while he washed away the barn dirt and smell. There were pork chops baked with gravy to cover the creamy mashed potatoes and towers of corn on the cob with newly picked squeaky green beans on the side. Huge ruby tomatoes had been sliced as salad and stacks of bread waited to mop up any leftover drops of grease.

In the lull after the bowls of food had been passed and everyone started to eat, Johnny blurted through a full mouth, "Wonder what Sam's up to now. What's the food like in the army?"

"Not as good as your mother's, from my experience," Lizzie's father replied.

"Do you think he'll call soon?" her mother asked softly, staring absently at the puddle of gravy and potato on her plate.

"He'll do it when he can."

Grandma Mary forced on a smile and passed the plate of corn. "Reminds me of when John went in," she said. "All you can do is wait. But he'll come through."

"Hasn't worked out well for the O'Neills, has it?" Lizzie's mother whispered. The room stilled.

Lizzie held her breath. They had not spoken about the incident in the park since the day it happened. There had been muted discussions between her parents, but never in front of her and her brothers.

"You got to trust Fred to the Lord," Grandpa Ernest said pragmatically. "Same for Sam. It's not up to us."

"Pretty different for Ray," Johnny exploded the silent subject. "Everyone's saying we're all to blame for Ray being in hospital."

There was a long moment as Grandpa Ernest drew a breath before answering. "If there's anyone to blame beside your Uncle Dan, it's me and your grandma. Not you, or your dad or mom."

He hesitated over the words. "I thought I was raising him right, but it doesn't seem to have taken."

Grandma Mary stretched her hand out over her husband's and gave a reassuring squeeze.

Images flashed across the screen of the muted television in the living room. Police confronted angry groups of black protesters just eight miles from the Convention Centre. A banner said men had died.

Lizzie picked up another ear of corn and rolled it over the butter. There was nothing better than fresh corn from the garden, she thought, as the butter smeared across her mouth and trickled down her wrists.   At the moment, it was all she could think about.

"How late are the speeches going to be?" Grandpa Ernest said changing the subject, glancing at the television. "I always hate it when it goes too late, but I want to hear what he's going to say."

"Don't worry," her father answered, "Nixon has promised to sort things out."

They had time for the apple pie with ice cream and for the dishes to be washed and put away before they all settled in front of the television for the closing night of the Convention. Their favourite son would accept the nomination to run for president.

"I pledge to you tonight that the first priority foreign policy objective of our next Administration will be to bring an honourable end to the war in Vietnam."

Lizzie thought his face was a little rat like, but she could see the hope in her mother's face when she heard those words. Lizzie preferred the voting night – it was much more fun. This long speech felt more like the minister's sermon on Sunday and she had to force herself to try and listen.

"How quickly do you think he could end the war?" her mother wanted to know.

"Not soon enough for Sam," her father warned.

Lizzie watched the hope drop from her mother's face and re-examined the man standing behind the podium on the television. Her parents were certain that the country would be better governed by him but she didn't understand how they could know that for sure. They wanted to believe he could end the war and bring peace to their streets. She wondered if he was able to keep the many promises he was making.

Suddenly the flash of car headlights bounced around the room and they heard a car pull up by the house.   Lizzie's parents gestured to each other, questioning who could be coming this late. Her mother pushed herself up from the chair to look out the window. Without a knock, the door burst open and a dishevelled Dan staggered into the room.

"Hi, all," he hiccupped before collapsing into a chair.

Grandpa Ernest shouted in anger, "You DROVE – again – when you've been drinking! Are you trying to kill someone – or yourself?"

Dan only rolled his head and smiled lopsidedly.

"You're a disgrace."

There was a movement by the door and it pushed open again. Lizzie squealed when she saw Sam's face peering through at them.

"It's okay, Grandpa, I drove him home."

Lizzie's mother raced to throw her arms around Sam, tracing his face with her hand in disbelief.

"How are you home?" she asked over and over.

"They gave me another deferment," Sam explained. "So I can go back to college. They dropped us off in town and I was about to call you when I saw Dan's car outside the bar across the parking lot."

"He's a good drinking buddy," Dan put in.

"Oh no," Grandma Mary said.

"I wasn't drinking," Sam was quick to assure her. "You know I'm not legal to drink yet anyway.   I just sat and listened – although he didn't make much sense -- and drank Coke until I could convince him to leave. I thought it would be safer if I drove instead of him."

"Thank you," Grandpa Ernest said simply. "I will take over now and drive him home this *last* time." He smiled at Sam. "I'm glad you're back."

Grandpa Ernest helped Dan to stand and put him in the passenger seat in the Rambler. Grandma Mary followed after giving Sam an extra hug and climbed into their Cadillac. The family watched the twin sets of tail lights run down the lane and the road toward town.

7 Sept 1968

Dad,

Mom said you wouldn't read my last letter. I hope you will read this one. You said you would never speak to me again and you were right to be angry. Don't blame Mom for wanting to see to me. It's my fault she's in this terrible place between you and me.

I know I went off the rails. I know it was wrong. I am sorry every day for what happened. I didn't mean to ruin anyone's life. It was more than an accident and the biggest mistake which I can never forget.

I let you down -- and Jackie. I am trying to make things right. Jackie has said we can start again and I want nothing more than to make it work with her. We've got little Sandy now and I need to be there for her and Simon.

You will be happy to hear I stopped drinking. And I won't drink again. It's become easier for me to walk down the street now and I hope it's better for you too. I didn't mean to bring shame on the family or you.

I want us to be a family. Can't you please forgive me?

Dan

5 August 2018

Elizabeth found the letter when she sat down at the desk to continue the search for Anna. She was wondering what to do with the box of Henry's letters . A couple of times, she had held her breath when Richard opened the sideboard to take something out. The thought of discovery worried at the back of her mind along with the shame that she was hiding them from Richard.

She had established sole control of her father's desk in a tacit agreement with Richard and decided Henry's box of letters would be safer in one of its long drawers. When she tried to slide the box to the back of the bottom drawer, she hit an obstruction. She pulled the drawer out as far as it would come and then reached back into its depths to pull out a small stationery box.

Lying on top inside was the small sealed envelope addressed to her grandfather. The smudged postmark said September 1968. Why had it been ignored and yet kept all these years, she wondered as her finger traced the edge of the flap. She was reluctant to read someone else's mail uninvited and felt the surge of protectiveness that shielded her own archived correspondence. But, she argued with her conscious, her grandparents and parents were now all gone and could not be embarrassed or angered by the letter's contents. Ignoring any breach of privacy, she slit open the flap.

The words baffled her. For years when they had family gatherings, Jackie brought Simon and Sandy and the grandparents were always pleased to see them. But Dan was never there. No one spoke about his absence and there was a unstated acceptance that he would never come to a family gathering. His name was rarely mentioned, but she had always had the impression that he chose to stay away. The guilt over the accident in the park had seemed a heavier penalty than the big fine and suspension of the driving licence for 6 months.

When she left for college her cousins were still young. She saw them briefly at Christmases and family reunions and funerals. There had been many funerals. Sandy had emailed she could not come to the one for Elizabeth's father as she had booked a trip to Europe nearly a year before and would be away then. Elizabeth almost felt relief since she had missed Dan's funeral when he died abruptly in a car crash 11 years ago. It seemed hypocritical to go to see him when he was dead after not seeing him for all those years when he was alive.

Elizabeth folded the letter back into its envelope and looked through the contents of the stationery box. A yellowed diploma showed her grandfather had graduated in 1922 from the same school as her father and herself. An article cut from the local paper reported on Grandpa Ernest's community work and his help in building the church.

There were copies of medical bills from the summer of 1968. She searched the form for the patient's name and was surprised to see Ray O'Neill's name. Why were these 50 year old documents stored in her father's desk, she wondered.

She picked through photos and the order of service from her grandparents' wedding and at the bottom of the box was a small book with worn corners. Opening it, she found it was a diary with just a handful of entries dated 1924. The script was scratchy and difficult to read. She picked through the uneven letters of the short inscriptions.

24 May 1924

Met up with Frank and walked over to see George. Mr O'Neill said he shouldn't come out with us, but he did anyway. Saturday night but no girls to see. Frank's got a bead on some 'shine.

26 May 1924

Missed church yesterday because my head hurt too much. Pa threatened to take a leather to me. Told him I was too old but he said I was a disgrace getting liquored like that. Should be arrested but I don't think he'll turn me in. Ma just said she'd pray even harder for me.

15 June 1924

Pa made me go to church cause I'd been missing too long. Met a new doll that's just moved into town who's the bees knees. Hope she'll go to the summer fair with me. George said he's getting a handcuff for Mitzy – he'll be manacled soon enough!

12 July 1924

Went out again with Mary. Third time this week. Her pa tells her not to. I gotta be on the straight and narrow or I won't be seeing her. George says he and Mitzy are planning a fall wedding. Won't be any nights out after that.

31 July 1924

Took Mary into Fenton. Farm Bureau are holding a square dance. Guess they're trying to get more members. Nothing better than swinging my gal and a kiss goodnight. Life's just jake.

The entries stopped and Elizabeth smiled at the teenage version of her grandfather. Grandpa Ernest had never been much of a writer. It surprised her that even these few entries had been made. It was equally surprising that the book remained in a box of documents left by him. She could only presume her father had discovered it when clearing his own parents' home and felt obliged to keep these scraps of family history.

This new glimpse of her grandfather was at odds with the conservative quiet man she had always known. She couldn't believe he had ever been drunk, and especially not during Prohibition. She wondered Grandma Mary was the reason he gave it up.

Her grandparents celebrated their golden wedding anniversary in December 1974. Elizabeth remembered there had been several such celebrations among that generation. She vaguely recalled George and Mitzy O'Neill held a party just a few weeks before her grandparents and it had been a source of sadness that her grandparents were not invited. She had not realised the friendship withdrawn after the accident at the park had such a long history.

She heard a click and the shush of the back door opening. Grabbing the box of Henry's letters, she slid them to the back of the bottom drawer, just before Richard appeared in the doorway.

"Working hard, I see," he said with a wide smile.

"You won't guess what I found in the desk." Elizabeth spread out her grandfather's papers across the desktop.

"What - they're your grandfather's?" Richard asked peering at the documents.

"I can tell you the day he met my grandma!" Elizabeth grinned, "It's in his diary, which I didn't even know he kept."

"Not much of one."

"More than I ever expected of him."

Richard read through the brief entries. "I love the lingo."

"You never think about your grandparents being young." Elizabeth paused. "What I can't understand is why he was so hard on Dan for drinking, when he obviously drank himself when it was actually illegal!"

"Was drinking the reason why he was shut out?" Richard cut to the heart of the problem.

"I always thought it was," Elizabeth said working through her memories of that summer. "He kept showing up drunk and then he just wasn't there any more. Grandma and Grandpa gave the impression that was the problem and that Dan just didn't come around because he wouldn't go along with Grandpa's rules."

"That's a long time to stay out of the family."

"It just became 'normal' '', Elizabeth admitted. "By the time you and I got together, he hadn't been coming to family parties for years and that's just the way it was."

"Anything else happen at that time?" Richard picked up the medical bills.

"There was this big accident once when Dan was drunk. Happened right in front of the whole church at a picnic. Dan came driving along, drunk, and hit one of the boys in JJ's class."

"Was it Ray?" Richard squinted at the hospital form.

"Yeah," Elizabeth confirmed. "He was the grandson of the George mentioned in the diary. He was hurt really bad – was in the hospital for a long time. The O'Neills never talked to us again after that."

"Why are the bills here then?"

Elizabeth sighed. "I really don't know. Were they trying to show how expensive it had been or did Grandpa pay the bills? Don't think Dan had much money.

Sandy was born a few weeks later and they were pretty strapped for cash."

"Surely someone knows what went on?"

"I don't think Sam or JJ do," Elizabeth said. "At least they've never said anything to me."

"Anyone else you can ask -- anyone coming to the sale?"

"The only ones left are Aunt Barbara who's out in Arizona – I don't expect her to fly in-- " Elizabeth answered, "and Jackie. She might come with Sandy or Simon. I wonder what she would say? How do I ask after all this time?"

"Maybe, it will just have to remain a mystery," Richard said as he headed off to their bedroom to change out of his office clothes.

Elizabeth reluctantly packed the documents into their box and nested it back in a desk drawer. The laptop blinked into life when she tapped it. She had several mysteries, she thought to herself, but she was getting better at solving them. She had tracked down Anna Myers to a small town near to the high school she had attended. Elizabeth's online investigations led to a diner. Her fingers hovered over the keys as she steeled herself to compose an email.

"Hello," she wrote. "I am looking for Anna Jackson who used to live in Clarksburg, IN, but moved away when she was 15. She was my friend then and I wanted to get in touch. If this is you, please email me back if you'd like to know what's happened in the past 50 years. Regards, Lizzie Williams."

Elizabeth winced at using the childhood moniker and quickly pressed 'send' before she could talk herself out of it.

9 August 1968

Sam drove Lizzie into Clarksburg to return her library book. The excitement of Sam's return prevented sleep and she had burrowed into her bed and read the final pages before closing her eyes. Sam's reward for returning home was to have the afternoon free from chores and he offered to drop Lizzie off on his way to see Glenda.

Sam pulled into a parking space just outside Harrison's store.

"Why don't we get a soda before you get your bike back?" Sam said generously.

Mr Harrison was re-arranging boxes of cereal on the shelf when they triggered the bell walking through the screen door. Sam nodded to the soda counter and Mr Harrison took up his place behind the gleaming taps of soft drinks.

"Sure you don't want something with that?" He asked as he pulled the first Coca Cola.

"Coke's enough today," Sam said, just as a woman emerged from the back aisle where rows of canned green beans and corn sat next to laundry detergent and batteries.

She stopped abruptly when she saw Sam and nearly dropped her basket of bread, eggs and flour.

"Hello, Mrs O'Neill," Sam edged off his bar stool to stand courteously.

"Thought you had been called up," she answered brusquely.

"The Army decided I wasn't good enough for them," Sam quipped with a hint of a smile.

"Not something to laugh about," rebuked Mrs O'Neill.

Sam ducked his head in contrition. "Sorry. I was just glad to be able to go back to college this fall."

There was an awkward pause where they looked at each other warily.

Finally Sam broke the impasse. "Can I ask how Ray is doing?"

Ruth O'Neill's long stare swept down and up his body before she replied. "No, I don't think you can," she said before abandoning her basket on the counter and striding out the screen door. She turned and looked back just as she reached the step down to the street and Lizzie thought she saw a tear track down her cheek.

Mr Harrison sighed as he picked the bread and eggs out of the basket to return to the shelves. "Think you need to tread carefully there," he cautioned Sam. "I've heard he may not ever walk properly again."

"I was only hoping that he was better," Sam defended.

They finished their drinks quickly and Sam got back into the car and waved goodbye as he drove away to see his girlfriend.

The bookmobile sat in the parking lot of the school. A mother and two young sons were boarding the vehicle when Lizzie arrived. She handed in *Airport* and had a quick look over the display of 'most popular picks'. She selected two quickly and the librarian casually stamped them with a return date while eying the boys pulling books from the shelves at the back of the bus.

Lizzie wrapped an arm around the books and held them firmly while meandering the short blocks to Anna's house. Even from a distance, Lizzie could see a change. There were large boxes sitting on the porch, rows of tools lining the path and piles of incomplete games and puzzles by the sidewalk with a sign saying 'free to take'.

Anna came out of the door carrying a box of dishes just as Lizzie reached the bottom step.

"Welcome to the crazy house," Anna said putting down the box.

"Looks like you're definitely leaving." Lizzie realised until this moment she had held onto a hope that they would change their plans and stay.

"Want any stuff?" Anna waved her arm towards the sidewalk mounds.

"I'm okay," Lizzie replied. "Good thing I came to get my bike before you gave that away as well!"

"Who's to say we haven't already?" Anna chided. "Don't worry, it's round the back."

Anna shifted a box of books out of the way so they could sit on the swing bench.

"I'm surprised they let you take that out," she said looking at Lizzie's top book.

"Mrs Zeller was too busy watching the Walton boys re-arranging the shelves to look at this." Lizzie slid *Rosemary's Baby* under the second book written by a popular Christian fiction author.

"Quite the combination in reading material" Anna joked.

"Figured if we couldn't go and see the film, I could just read it instead, " Lizzie hesitated, "although maybe not last thing at night. I think *Christy* is better for bedtime!"

The chains on the bench creaked gently as they pushed back at the same time with their feet to rock the seat slightly.

"Wish we didn't have to go." A seriousness settled into Anna's face.

"Then stay," Lizzie said simply.

"It's not possible." Anna stared at her hands resting in her lap. "Everything's been decided and we've got the movers coming on Monday."

"What's your new school like?"

"Oh," Anna replied, "it's just a school. Nothing special."

"You'll have a whole other set of seniors to sort out!" Lizzie tried to lighten the mood.

"That's not helping," Anna protested but gave a weak smile.

"Anna," her mother called from inside the house, "can you come and get the box of books from the living room?" She appeared at the door and looked about to say something more when she saw Lizzie sitting next to Anna.

"I didn't know you were here, Lizzie," she said. "Sorry about the mess, but this is what it's like when you move. Would you like a drink before you take the bike home?"

Lizzie shook her head, feeling that she was an obstacle to be worked around.

"Didn't mean to get in the way," she apologised

"I'm sorry to hurry you, but we've got so much to get done and I do need Anna to help."

"Mom," Anna protested, "just give us a few minutes, please?"

Her mother held her gaze for a moment and then retreated inside.

"She's just stressed," Anna said. "It's all been a rush. Dad's still finishing off at his job, so it's just us doing most of the packing."

"Do you want some help?" Lizzie offered trying to delay her departure.

"Thanks, but we'll manage."

"Maybe I can come down sometime and see you?" Lizzie asked hopefully.

Anna smiled. "I'd like that. I'll have to send you the address – I haven't learned it yet myself!"

Lizzie stood slowly, wanting to hold onto the moment of parting for as long as possible. They walked around the house and found the bike leaning against the cellar doors. Lizzie placed her new library loans into the basket and took hold of the handlebars to guide the bike as they walked out to the street.

"You gonna be at church on Sunday?" Lizzie asked.

Anna shook her head. "We're going up to spend the day with grandma and grandpa before we move. They're not happy that we will be so much further away."

"So this is it?"

"Afraid so," Anna said, biting her lip. "I *will* miss you."

"Me too," was all Lizzie could say. "Me too."

She straddled the bike and slowly pushed the pedal down to propel the bike forward. It wobbled as she turned to look back at her friend for one last time. Anna stood watching – her shoulders dropping like the curve of her down turned mouth. She gave a final wave as Lizzie turned the corner at the end of the street.

Lizzie felt the wetness on her cheeks and tried to brush it away with her sleeve while she rode through the town. When the road shifted from tarmac into gravel and the houses became sparse, she let the tears run unchecked. She rode through a blurry landscape numbly avoiding the road's potholes by instinct.

At the end of their lane, she found the mail and the newspaper still in their boxes and added them to her basket. Her mother was weeding the flower beds by the house and got up from her kneeling position to greet her.

"You look hot," she said taking in Lizzie's red face, but ignoring the tear tracks.

"Just as well I got the bike back before someone else got it." Lizzie rested the bike against the hickory tree. "They're going on Monday. Just like that."

"I'm sorry, Lizzie," her mother told her. "They have to do what's best and I guess this is it. I know it's hard on you, but that's what life is like sometimes."

Lizzie collected the books and mail from the basket and slid *Rosemary's Baby* to the bottom so her mother wouldn't see it. She handed over the letters and newspaper and headed toward the house.

"Oh no."

Lizzie turned to see her mother reading the front page of the newspaper.

"It's Fred O'Neill," she explained. "He's a prisoner in some Vietnamese camp."

"At least he's alive," Lizzie said hopefully.

"Not by much, from what I've heard of those camps," her mother replied. "Oh, poor Ruth."

Lizzie remembered their encounter with Mrs O'Neill. "She was at Harrison's this afternoon. Sam and I got a soda and she was there. She seemed angry at Sam. Guess this explains why."

Her mother took a deep breath. "All the more reason to hate us. What with Ray and everything. She's put the phone down every time I've tried to call her since the picnic."

She stared vacantly out over the fields. Lizzie thought her mother seemed to shrink with sorrow. Ruth O'Neill had been her friend as long as Lizzie could remember. Lizzie wanted to take her mother's hand and say she understood how it felt to have friendship stripped away for no reason that you could control – to be abandoned at the whim of fate. But before she could speak, her mother straightened and smiled wanly.

"I suppose we had better see what we can do for supper, Lizzie," she said as she turned back toward the house.

1 May 1973

Ma cherie Lizzie,

I am still blown away by your visit. I couldn't believe you were standing on my doorstep. It was just WAY OUT. It was so incredible that my head has nearly exploded. I am trying to remember what we talked about but it's buried under the shock of meeting I think.

I wish you hadn't had to return to university so soon. I needed time to calm down before we could talk properly so my poor brain could take it in.

Susan keeps telling her friends how amazing the night was and Geoff and Daniel have been asking after you (and Helen) as well. I think Geoff fancies Helen! Do you think she feels the same way? We're all trying to work out how we can afford to come and see you! (We are only poor students! But that is no excuse when you came to see us!)

When does your term finish? Would you be able to come back to Leeds? My year ends in four weeks. But then I've got some end of year papers to finish as well. When are you going back to the US? I wish we could have come to Indiana years ago when we moved as I wanted to see your farm after all that you have told me about it.

Can you write back ASAP?

Ta ami toujours,
Henry

14 August 2018

    The excitement bouncing from the letter kept ricocheting in her mind as she tried to focus on her driving. She had been slowly going back through Henry's letters so she could fully absorb their contents, following only a hasty look at them earlier in the summer.

    She and Helen nearly danced their way back to Paris at the end of their visit to Leeds. There had been a touch of magic about the evening, but once they were back in their student apartment, they were unsure whether they had only imagined the feeling. This letter had been their confirmation. Elizabeth smiled at the memory.

    The road was misted by soft rain and Elizabeth blocked out the charges exploding inside her to concentrate on the passing cars. She breathed deep and released the air slowly for calm. Her hands were aching from their tight grip of the steering wheel for the past hour. She should not have started this trip with the clench in her stomach from Richard's refusal to come with her. It had been many years since she had looked after a child on her own and it would have been so much easier with the two of them. Dave had a meeting he needed to attend in North Carolina and Kiera asked if they could babysit overnight so she could go with him.

    After caring for Zoe, Elizabeth had hoped for a romantic weekend with Richard in the mountains. It felt like a long time since they had changed the pattern of their day to day, even if only briefly. Life seemed to be captured in a hamster wheel of replication and at moments she felt weighed down by its ordinariness. She had hoped with more time together in retirement they could explore the dreams they had when they were young, have adventures and challenge themselves.

But at the last moment, Richard said he couldn't go – there was a project he couldn't leave.

"You're supposed to be retired," she had shouted.

He had replied with a hopeless shrug.

"You're part-time," she continued. "You can get someone else to cover."

Richard half smiled at her but shook his head. There was no one, he said, but she could see that distance behind the eyes that came when he was working through a technical problem. She had never been able to compete when his thoughts were centred on solving the jigsaw of circuits that made the computer systems work. When they first met, his passion seemed endearing, but Elizabeth discovered it was more competition than any woman. She had learned to resign herself to the absences when something came up at work, but occasionally the desire to be first boiled up.

She hadn't wanted to admit to nervousness in looking after Zoe. Richard was always so natural in scooping up his granddaughter when she needed attention. Elizabeth felt less sure. It had been over 30 years since she had been responsible for a baby. Friends told her how they enjoyed being grandparents and it was even better than having your own, but Elizabeth thought the duty of care must be even greater when you had to hand your charge back to someone else to assess your proficiency. She loved her granddaughter more fully than she had expected, but that made her need to do it well all the more acute.

The sign for her exit off the freeway grew out of the distance and she pulled the car over to the right lane. She took another deep breath and relaxed her hands. The car rolled onto the exit ramp and Kiera's house was just twenty minutes away.

Dave was loading their car when Elizabeth arrived.

"Thought Richard was coming as well," he said as she emerged from the driver's seat.

"So did I," she replied with a slightly rictus smile. "Last minute hiccup with work."

Kiera appeared at the door with Zoe in her arms.

"We need to get going or I'm going to be late for my own talk at this rate," Dave told her with an accusatory glance at Elizabeth. The argument with Richard had made her late.

"Sorry to rush, Mom," Kiera said, "but can you take Zoe so I can get my handbag?"

The chubby infant was thrust onto her grandmother.

"I thought there would be an induction," Elizabeth complained, "before you rushed off."

"Oh," Dave joked, "You know what to do. And Kiera's been leaving notes all over the house, so you can't go wrong."

Zoe reached for a wisp of silver hair as Elizabeth kissed her soft head but then was distracted by a large button on her grandmother's blouse. Elizabeth shifted the weight in her arms for a better hold.

The screen door banged behind Kiera as she returned to the car. Elizabeth saw the glow of escape on her face and remembered how excited she had been the first time she and Richard had a night away from childcare. Kiera had been nearly six months old when his mother agreed to babysit over a weekend. The joy of being themselves and not just parents had been intoxicating even before a glass of wine.

Dave quickly hauled Elizabeth's overnight bag from the car and dropped it in the living room before they were suddenly gone. The house seemed hollow and Zoe became restless. Elizabeth propped her in her baby seat and walked around the kitchen reading the post-it note instructions papering the cupboards. Her confidence was battered by each missive as it appeared her daughter doubted her ability to cope without very detailed guidance.

"What do you think, Zoe?" She said to break the quiet. "Will you help me out?"

Zoe stared back blankly and kicked her feet to make the seat jiggle.

"I will take that as a 'yes'," Elizabeth said putting water on to boil for a cup of coffee.

They sat on the small screened porch as the morning cleared into streaks of sunshine and the clouds rolled away. Elizabeth teased Zoe with plastic rattles and soft animals and they watched as squirrels raced each other across the lawn.

At mid-day, she searched in the fridge and found leftover pasta to microwave and a bottle to warm. Zoe guzzled down the milk until her eyelids began to droop and her lips relaxed, releasing the bottle's teat. Elizabeth gently raised the limp body to her shoulder and patted Zoe's back until a soft belch emerged. She cradled the baby into her cot and sat back with a sigh of relief. Childcare felt more demanding than she remembered: or, she thought to herself, is she just getting old?

The day was heating up again and Elizabeth was happy to sit in the shade of the porch eating her lunch. There was little movement on the suburban street. She watched a delivery van edge past cautiously as the driver read the house numbers before stopping and getting out to hand over a package. There were distant screams of children and the sound of splashing coming from a few houses down the street.

The scene felt familiar and she realised it was an echo of her own life when Kiera was a baby. During the early years of their marriage, they had lived on a similar street where the family homes were separated by narrow driveways. On hot summer days, she would spread a quilt under the shade of their ancient apple tree and Kiera would doze while Elizabeth read the current best seller.

She remembered the long days of isolation, stretched by repetition and boredom, as she waited for Richard to return home from work. It had taken time to find the toddler groups and the mothers who would become friends. She had craved release from the days of doldrums, but looking back Elizabeth shuddered with the speed at which the intervening years had disappeared.

There was a snuffling sound from the cot and Zoe's mouth suckled as she slept.

Elizabeth shook her head to dispel the past. There was time, while Zoe slept, to catch up on the present. She slipped into the living room, pulled her laptop out of the overnight bag and settled back on the porch where there was a light breeze. She was pleased to see new emails waiting for her and surprised to find one from Helen.

Ever since sharing an apartment as students in Paris, they kept in touch spasmodically over the years. Helen had been the bold adventurer who spurred her into visiting Henry. She travelled the world after university, working for NGOs in developing countries, and Elizabeth found in her stories from different countries a life she wished she had been brave enough to try. Setting up schools in Uganda or clean water projects in India had been an exotic contrast to her years spent mashing baby food, repeatedly reading Kiera's two favourite books and playing hide and seek in a suburban garden.

"Happy very belated birthday," the email began. "Hope it went well. Sorry to be so late. Can't say I appreciate the extra years. We're a long way from our student days. Wish I was still young enough to go hitching around England like we did. Mind you, I don't think the kids do that any more either! I don't have the children to warn not to do it, but I don't imagine Kiera would have tried it. Have you ever told her about your escapades when we were young?"

Elizabeth laughed and agreed that some things were best kept to yourself.

"Sadly, I am finally reaching that point where I need to retire, but I don't know where to do it! I have travelled so much that I don't know what feels like home now. Not sure where to set up permanentl - or where I fit in. If you've got any suggestions, let me know. Helen."

It wasn't just another time period, Elizabeth thought. She must have been a different person, remembering the excitement coming from the letter Henry wrote after they met. She had never inspired such elation before or since. Had it just been a bubble of the moment? The year as a student abroad not only separated her from her country, it pushed her into new ways of thinking about herself and what she could do. It had been up to her to use the experience as expansively as possible and she wondered if she had failed to use it fully. She came home, excited and challenged, but bit by bit she returned to the same life that led her to sit here mourning who she had become.

Henry had only been a moment in her life. She knew that. The promises to meet again failed under the weight of course work and obligations. Writing his final essays meant Henry didn't travel to Paris and Elizabeth's plans to travel Europe were cut short when her parents decided to celebrate their silver wedding anniversary in early June. The moment was there and lost.

The humid afternoon pressed down heavily. Elizabeth stared down the street but saw lush dark greens of a wet England rather than the yellowing brown grass of summer. She could still sense his intense gaze and felt the wash of his wide smile flood over her. Taking a deep calming breath, she pulled up a search page on the laptop and typed in Henry's name.

A directory service provided a list of possibilities. She looked through the addresses and examined the map around Leeds for towns and villages. Suddenly, she found an entry for a hamlet on the outskirts of Leeds. The age guideline read 60-70. A flip of her stomach made her certain this was the right one. Another person lived at this address. Was Robin McKinley his partner or wife? She wondered how long they had been together and what she was like. A tincture of jealousy prodded Elizabeth to hope Robin might be a version of herself that he had as a substitute, but then she tucked the thought away deep in her mind for being inappropriate. She was being foolish. She knew it, but couldn't stop her need to know more.

She returned to the directory and scrolled through the entries. Earlier entries showed only Henry's name at this address. Robin appeared to have moved in in 2006, but Henry lived there before. Were they married? She didn't know why it would matter, but felt compelled to find out. She googled how to find a marriage certificate and came up with a website where she could apply for one. She quickly filled in the form to look for a certificate for an unknown date of marriage in or around 2006, hesitated only briefly before paying a substantial fee on their joint credit card and closed the website before rationality returned.

Elizabeth snapped the laptop shut and vaulted to her feet. A fizz of anxiety jolted through her. She paced the five steps across the porch back and forth trying to release the sudden energy. It had been a mistake but she couldn't stop it now. Curiosity was said to kill a cat, but she believed the same might also now be true for her as well. She sucked in a long breath and held it to settle the fluttering in her chest.

Zoe kicked in her cot. An arm reached out and Elizabeth could see that she was waking. She was too old to be so reckless, she told herself, and yet, she wondered if

Henry had children and if he was a grandfather? Did he have a small child he held and told stories to about a girl he once met?

Zoe stared at her, confused in her sleepiness.

"You want your mommy, don't you?" Elizabeth soothed. She gathered up the baby to distract herself from the gnaw of growing apprehension and made cooing sounds as she refreshed the diaper before settling Zoe into the pushchair for a long walk around the neighbourhood.

27 August 1968

The house fell suddenly silent as Lizzie was left on her own. After the slapping of the suitcase down the stairs and the shouting as Johnny raced back to his room to check that everything had been packed, the quiet felt misplaced.

Breakfast had been a loud and chaotic meal. Johnny was pulsing with the adventure of leaving home. The summer abruptly ended when the moment came for him to leave for orientation at college. It still surprised Lizzie that he had gotten into Purdue University although it was sensible he was pursuing studies in agriculture. The freshmen had five days on campus before the rest of the students returned and Johnny had spent the previous two days picking through the lists of things he needed to take and gathering them in piles on his bedroom floor. Lizzie couldn't see how it would all fit into their car, but then the piles became compressed into suitcases or boxes which were shoved into the corners of the car trunk and piled onto half of the back seat, leaving just enough room for her mother to wedge in her legs.

Her mother had prepared Johnny's favourites for breakfast: waffles with deep pockets oozing with maple syrup, soft poached eggs sitting on corned beef hash, juicy sliced peaches and fresh donuts from the bakery if a final treat was needed.

The radio played in the background spilling out news from the Democratic Convention in Chicago. They had held their breath a few days before when they heard the city's police raided nearby black neighbourhoods. The newsman said it was to prevent an assassination attempt on Hubert Humphrey, one of the candidates running for president, but they remembered the riots and violence which had erupted in cities across the country after Martin Luther King Jr was killed in April and were afraid it could happen again.

"I'm so glad you didn't choose college in Chicago," their mother fretted as they listened to reports of student demonstrations near the convention centre.

"They're not just from Chicago," Sam warned. "They're coming from all over to protest against the war."

"Yeah," said Johnny, "did you hear that guy who said if you're going to the Chicago you need to wear some armour in your hair?"

"It's not going to be like San Francisco in the song," Sam agreed, "that's for sure."

The announcer on the radio continued with his report, "Mayor Daley has called in 6,000 National Guardsmen to keep order as thousands demonstrate outside the convention centre."

"Wonder who's going to be chosen as their candidate," John Sr mused. "Kennedy would probably have won."

"I'd vote for Pigasus," Johnny laughed. "Did you see the pig the Yippies were going to nominate? Too bad the police stopped them before getting inside."

Their mother frowned. "I don't want you two getting into any of these protests."

"It's called student power, Mom," Sam said. "It's all over the world. We see we have a voice and we want to use it."

"You heard what that Abbi Hoffman said," their father argued. "They said they'd put LSD in the convention centre's water and try and seduce the delegates and their wives and daughters! That's not protest. That's anarchy."

"Someone's got to make them change their minds on the War," Sam countered. "We've been lucky so far – Johnny and I could still get called up. Unless we make them change their policy, we could end up just like the O'Neills – or worse."

"It's got to be Nixon, then," their mother said softly. "He promised to end it."

Lizzie had stared out the window as the sea of debate roiled around her. A light breeze rippled through a field of corn. A cow grazing in the pasture flicked flies with her tail. A milk truck spewed up dust as it visited farms down the road. The only agitation in the rural landscape came from the images in her mind of guardsmen with guns pushing back protesters hundreds of miles away, but it coloured the calm with darkness.

A new voice took over the radio as the programme shifted back to music. Breathlessly, he announced the next track as the day-old release of the Beatles' new song 'Hey, Jude'. Johnny's forkful of egg stopped mid-flight to his mouth as he strained to listen.

"Shush," he quelled the discussion. Sam and Lizzie sat attentively through the plaintive lyrics while their parents continued eating and rolling their eyes at each other. When the song moved into the long repetitive na, nah, na, na, nah, na, her mother pulled back from the table and took her plate to the bowl of kitchen waste to scrape off the remains as the teenagers sang along softly.

As the music ended, Lizzie looked at her brothers and smiled. A new Beatles song always topped anything else.

"Well, that makes it 11 minutes past nine," the radio voice returned. "Time to get a look at prices over at the farmers' auction this morning."

"Now we're running late," her mother barked, flicking the radio off. "Finish quickly. Lizzie can do the dishes. We need to get going."

There was an abrupt end to the meal and Johnny rushed to squeeze the last items into the car. In their haste, her parents rowed over where the map had been left and where they would all sit. Lizzie followed the trio out to the car and waved goodbye as they headed down the drive, but Johnny didn't look back.

The screen door slammed behind her as she returned to the kitchen and slid back into her chair at the table. She surveyed the abandoned plates slicked with grease and drops of egg and the pans left unscraped on the stove. She sighed and pushed back the lid of the bakery box to find an iced, cream-filled donut. She inhaled the caramel scent and then bit down into the sweet goo.

"Looks like you get to eat all of those," Sam said behind her making her jump. His hair was still damp from the shower and he left a trail of High Karate cologne as he brushed by her.

"You don't want any?" Lizzie asked through a mouthful of soft dough.

"They're all yours. I'm off to see Glenda. – I'll be back for milking. Mom and Dad said they'd be home late."

Before she could ask anything else, Sam was gone. Lizzie heard the pickup truck start and the crunch of gravel as it left. She took another bite of the donut and let the filling ooze around her mouth. A day of solitude and five more donuts lay ahead of her.

Lizzie filled the sink with hot water and cleared the plates from the table into it. When she turned to the stove, her heart sank at seeing so many pans with remnants of hardened food and bowls holding spoonsful of batter. She reached past the dirtied bowls on the table and plucked off the box of donuts which she placed next to her new library book on the coffee table in the living room. Lizzie pulled the table a little closer to the couch and checked the box was within reach before plumping the cushions and laying down with her feet propped on the arm rest.

The bookmobile had returned on Friday, but Lizzie hadn't had time to read the new selections over the weekend. She certainly wouldn't be interrupted now, she thought as she stared at the cover of *The Spy Who Came in From the Cold.* She felt it had been a topical choice. Just two days before, the news had been full of the Prague invasion with streets overrun by Russian tanks brought in to suppress liberal reforms started in the spring. The battle with communism didn't seem that cold to Lizzie. Vietnam was supposed to be about defeating communism and that was certainly a hot war zone. Even discussing what to do about the War caused fights: the images of guardsmen confronting students in Chicago flashed again through her mind. Lizzie wedged open the book, stretched out her arm and pulled another donut from the box as she settled down to read.

After a couple of chapters, she lay the book on her chest. The story of British double agents reminded her that Henry was now living in England. She wondered what the country was like. His postcard from London was the last she had heard from him and that was only to say he had arrived. If he stopped writing now, she wouldn't even know where he was. Her thoughts shifted to Anna and she realised the same was true of her. In the rush to move, Anna had never told her where they were moving to or given her an address. She promised to write or phone, but although Lizzie expectantly searched through every bundle of mail, there was never anything from her.

The house was so quiet. She could even hear the soft ticking of the mantle clock that was normally drowned by Johnny's incessant quips. By next week, Sam will have returned to college as well, she thought, and it will be just her with her parents. Her dad will fall asleep in the chair early in the evening and her mother will have no one to fret over because Lizzie won't be able to go out on her own. She wasn't old enough to drive. And, she realised, she had no one to go and see anyway.

She closed her eyes and tried to squeeze out the image of the three of them sitting here every night for the next two years until she left for college. Dogs barked in the distance and a truck rumbled down the road. She felt the emptiness of being alone and reached for another donut.

8 September 1968

Dear Lizzie,

It has been crazy this past month. Sorry not to write sooner. The trip to get here seemed to take forever – we had so many stops along the way. Did you get my postcards? I think I will have to go back some day to all the cities where we stopped. Obviously we couldn't go and see everything as we were just catching connection flights.

Although I was excited about coming to England, I can tell YOU I was nervous as well. I had only lived in Singapore and didn't know if I would like it here. But I DO! It's very different. Leeds is a much smaller city than Singapore and you can quickly get out to the countryside.

That's the part I like best. It's so green everywhere. We didn't have the fields and farms in Singapore. It looks completely DIFFERENT. But, I suppose you are used to being on a farm. I will send you some photos when I get my film developed. I took some of the farms we saw because I thought you would be interested.

A lot of the fields are surrounded by stone walls or really high hedges. It's scary driving down the country lanes because there's only room for one car, but the traffic goes BOTH WAYS! There are high hedges on both sides and it's like being in a tunnel. Is that what it is like in Indiana? Maybe you can send me pictures of your farm so I can see what it's like.

School has started and I am getting to know my classmates. They think I am a bit strange, having come from abroad, but hopefully they will get used to me. It's going to be hard to begin with because I need to catch up with where they are on my subjects.

Please keep on writing to me. I haven't heard from any of my friends from Singapore yet. I hope they won't forget me.
Ta amie toujours,

Henry

21 August 2018

Elizabeth punched off the power button on the TV's remote controller. She felt exhausted from the news. It had been a double hitter day with the President's personal lawyer admitting he brokered payments at the request of Donald Trump to pay off women making sexual allegations. The chairman for the Trump campaign in 2016 had also been convicted on eight counts of fraud. She couldn't believe how many scandals flowed out of one presidency.

It was nearly six o'clock, but she didn't know if it was worth starting to cook. Richard hadn't said when he would be home and she was reluctant to spoil another dinner trying to keep it warm. They hadn't spoken to each other much since she returned from babysitting Zoe. Initially, Elizabeth had been glad work was keeping him busy as she felt an edge of guilt after applying for Henry's marriage certificate. It was information she didn't need but had been propelled against logic to get. Her secret lay between them but Richard was too preoccupied to notice and she had been grateful for that.

As the week passed, the irritation of guilt was covered by increasing layers of frustration and then anger at Richard's continuing late night work sessions. Two nights ago, she had called him up to find out when he would be back. She meant to be polite, but he was vague and refused to say how long he would be.

"Come home, now," she demanded.

"What's wrong?" Richard sounded concerned.

"I'm tired of eating on my own," she had whined, knowing it made her sound pathetic.

"I can't," he said. "We're right in the middle of it and can't stop at the moment."

She had slammed the phone down, perhaps harder than she intended. She took her lasagne to the conservatory and ate against the backdrop of a setting sun and a deepening twilight. It was nearly 11 o'clock when Richard finally arrived. The growing resentment choked calm conversation and Elizabeth had avoided another confrontation by taking a book to bed.

She was still struggling to read it. After looking at it most of the afternoon, she was just midway through the third chapter. The quiet evening lay oppressively around her, only broken by distant calls of children playing down the street. She wished she could have a glass of chilled Pinot Grigio and release her moanings to Grace, but she and Bob had headed to the beach for two weeks to escape the August heat. They weren't the only neighbours missing in the road. Elizabeth counted four other homes she knew where the families were away on vacation.

"Having fun," she grumped with jealousy to herself.

Travel magazines taunted her from the side table. They were heavily thumbed and corners of pages were turned down on her favourite destinations. There were so many places she had wanted to see, but somehow there had always been a reason to put it off: a baby, work, school schedules, expense. Not that they hadn't gone on vacations – they had memories of weeks at the beach, of hikes through the Appalachian mountains, of jazz in New Orleans and visits to Disneyworld. Maintaining her French for translation work meant a trip to Quebec every few years. She loved rambling around the Lower Town, visiting art and craft galleries and savouring French cuisine, but the trips had fallen into familiarity and were no longer adventures in new experiences.

Their trip to Europe three years ago had been the first excursion out of North America since her student days in Paris. It had lacked the rawness of youth but it reached some of her dreams. She could now compete on the list of 100 best places to visit at suburban dinner parties. They had seen the Coliseum, the canals of Venice, the Tyrol mountains and the Brandenburg Gate, but they felt like stamps on a tourist's bingo card. There had been no time to wallow in the culture or to roam the narrow back alley ways of Paris.

When she and Helen were students there, they used to spend entire afternoons cosseting cups of coffee at sidewalk cafes watching people passing while writing their fictional lives. They would wander through the markets, collecting tomatoes, cheeses and bread to eat in their small apartment. On Sundays they would watch the streams of couples brandishing bouquets intended for the mothers who were preparing large family dinners.

On the tour there had been no opportunity to be languorous. Breaks for coffee were timed and filled with maps and postcards -- not wistful longings to immerse themselves among the locals. They had raced around Europe for two and a half weeks and returned home drained. Richard hated being corralled by the tour leader and led in a long group around the historic sites. By the time they got to London, the last stop on the tour, they were ready to break away and wander the streets on their own. As a result, Elizabeth thought, they enjoyed London the most. But like every other stop, there wasn't time to venture beyond the city and Elizabeth really wanted to see the English countryside. She reread Henry's descriptions of the fields and lanes and wished they had seen them. As they flew home, they had looked down at the patchwork of hedge-lined fields expanding beyond the urban developments and she promised to return.

Could she have chosen to live in England if life had been different, she wondered. Helen opted for a life abroad but now needed to choose a home. She had always written with such passion about each country where she lived. Elizabeth stretched and moved to the desk to check for any updates from Helen. As she waited for the laptop to boot up, she watched a squirrel dart across the lawn, its mouth distended with the prize it was taking to hide.

The laptop screen glowed on and she scanned through the unopened emails but didn't see anything from Helen. Mostly there were emails from subscriber services that she kept forgetting to cancel. Her eyes caught on one from 'amyers0432' which just read 'Hello' in the subject line. She was about to delete it as an unknown contact when she suddenly realised it was from Anna. Her finger trembled slightly as she clicked to open the email.

"Lizzie, it was a surprise (but a good one) to hear from you. As you have worked out, I have a café, although my daughter is gradually taking it over as I slow down. It's hard to know where to start. I would love to know what you have done over the past 50 years. I don't seem to have moved much after leaving Clarksburg. I've been here at the café flipping burgers for 30 years. I am sure you have had a more exciting life.

"It's hard to know what to say in an email. It would be much better to meet. Where are you living? Do you get back to Indiana very often? Maybe you could come visit? There's so much to talk about but I just can't put it into an email.

"I'm hoping you can visit soon.   Anna"

Elizabeth stared at the writing trying to pick through its sparse layers. She agreed talking was easier than correspondence, so she quickly sent a reply saying she would be going to the farm auction and could travel down to see her the day after.

1 September 1968

It was the last Sunday of summer. Lizzie hadn't wanted to go to church, but knew there was no excuse her parents would accept. She particularly wanted to avoid the Sunday school class. The awkward teenage boys would cluster on one side of the circle of chairs, attempting rough flirtations with the girls opposite them. Sitting next to Anna or Johnny, she had found a place at the edge of the groupings. Entering the room alone, Lizzie hesitated, unsure where to sit.

Emily, Diane and Joanna were posturing as they gossiped, casting sly glances to see if the boys were looking their way. The three had said they were sorry Anna moved away, but Lizzie could see they revelled in the new opportunities. Anna had always drawn the boys' attention with her long silky hair that glowed when caught by sunlight. The trio had resented Anna's easy attraction and Lizzie was an unwelcome reminder of someone they would prefer to forget.

Letting the clatter of conversation swirl around her, Lizzie took a back row seat in the unclaimed area between the two groups. She pretended to study the points of today's lesson set out on their weekly leaflet. Jonah and the whale was the subject for discussion and she could now imagine how it felt to be swallowed whole and not be able to escape.

A sudden hush in the room made Lizzie look up. The knot of teenage boys by the entrance unravelled to allow through a pale figure supported by a crutch. His gray green eyes seem to hunt the room before fixing Lizzie to her spot. She felt a warmth rising up her neck and dropped her gaze back to the lesson on Jonah. There was a squeal of metal pushed across the concrete floor and a thud as Ray O'Neill dropped heavily onto a seat. The clamour of voices returned in a swift wave and Lizzie winced as she heard the creak of the chairs as bodies shifted away from her.

Mrs Foster finally entered and called the class to order. She asked them to open their bibles and heads poured over the small print under her strict command. Lizzie couldn't focus the blurred words to read the verses. When the teacher asked her what God had asked Jonah to do, she froze and her mind went blank. When she didn't get an answer, Mrs Foster moved on to Diane who tossed her hair and smiled.

"He was supposed to go to Ninevah and tell them how bad they were," she said to the group. "But," she added, "he ran away. He was too scared."

The words felt barbed and struck Lizzie like a physical assault. No one at the church had spoken to her about the accident at the picnic and she had hidden from the topic because there was so much bad feeling against the family. It wasn't going to disappear, she recognised, especially with Ray sitting in the class circle. She ventured a sweeping glance in his direction and found the gray green eyes still locked on her.

Mrs Foster continued talking, but it was just a background of sound that Lizzie couldn't understand. Although the class settled into analysing the meaning of the story, Lizzie felt more distanced with each word. By the end of the session, all she wanted was to run from the room and avoid all the unasked questions.

In the crush of teens filing out into the hall, Lizzie suddenly came face to face with Ray.

"Glad you're getting better," she managed to say.

"I'm really mad at Johnny," was Ray's reply. "What's up with him?"

"What do you mean?" Lizzie felt the ground shift and tilt beneath her.

"He didn't even say goodbye before he went off to college." Ray leaned closer. "Can't believe he just went away like that."

"Oh."

"You just tell him I want to hear what he's getting up to, will ya?" Ray hobbled ahead and was swallowed in the tide of church members flowing into the sanctuary for the service.

The surprise of his comment lingered until later when her family was gathered around the fold out picnic table on Grandma Mary and Grandpa Ernest's lawn. Lizzie thought it was a perfect day for the last picnic of the season. The humid summer had dropped away over the Labour Day weekend, preparing for the change into autumn.

Her father, Uncle Joe and Grandpa Ernest worked the burgers on the flimsy barbecue. Barbara and Charlotte helped carry out bowls of potato salad and coleslaw to the table while Tom tried to ignore the screams of the twins as they raced each other to the barn and back.

Sam was buried behind the news pages of the Indianapolis Star which he bought at Harrisons store after church. The flood of the remaining sections of the Sunday newspaper splayed across his lap and the ground. Lizzie grabbed the advertising inserts with their numerous offers and coupons and anchored them with a flower pot to prevent them blowing away in the light breeze. She pulled out the comics section and smiled at its pristine condition – Johnny normally got it first and she received the dishevelled sheets when he was finished reading.

"Ray seemed angry at Johnny," Lizzie said to Sam.

"Didn't think the O'Neills were talking to us," Sam replied behind the newspaper.

"Neither did I. He was kind of glaring at me during Sunday School."

"Sounds more like it."

"But then he said he was mad at Johnny because he left without saying goodbye."

The newspaper came crunching down and Sam appeared from behind it.

"That's good, then, isn't it?" he asked. "At least maybe he doesn't blame us."

"Blame who?" Their mother had walked up to the table with a hot casserole of baked beans.

"Ray's been asking after Johnny," Sam explained. "At least he's talking to us."

"That's a good thing, then." But Lizzie saw a tightness at the corners of her mother's mouth. "I wish Ruth felt the same."

"About what?" Grandma Mary asked as she arrived with a stack of buns and condiments for the burgers.

"Ruth's still won't talk to me after the accident."

"Mitzy's the same way with me," Grandma Mary admitted. She sighed. "Guess we might feel that way if it had been Sam or Johnny who'd been hurt. But, we can't change what's done now, so we just have to hope time will heal."

Grandpa Ernest came up behind his wife carrying a plate of cooked burgers.

"We've done all we could," he said. "It's up to them to accept and move forward."

With that, the subject was closed down as the family pulled their chairs around the table and settled down to eat. The twins held their giggling while everyone bowed their heads for Grandpa Ernest's blessing on the food and then grabbed for the same burger on the plate as soon as 'Amen' was uttered. Barbara smacked back their hands while reaching for the platter to pass it around.

Lizzie loved the swirl of passing bowls and the clamour to fill your plate as quickly as possible. It was followed by the hiatus when everyone settled into eating. Only after the gnaw of hunger had been given a few spoonfuls of food did conversation re-start. Lizzie was happy to let it wash over her as she concentrated on her mounds of creamy potato salad and sticky baked beans.

Joe started describing the extension he and Charlotte wanted to build on their house. Grandpa Ernest discussed milk prices with her father and Lisa and Laura stared at Lizzie as they munched through their burgers.

It felt like a perfect afternoon, but the absences pierced the bubble of contentment, letting out the pleasure as the skim of reality tightened around them. Johnny was gone. By next week, Sam would also have left for college. Lizzie wondered if Dan would ever be allowed to return to the family. There was a moment's pause in the conversation.

"If Ray isn't mad at us over the accident," Lizzie dropped into the moment. "Maybe Dan could say sorry and we could all be friends again?"

She felt backs stiffen around her, locking into rigid postures. No one looked at her, but there were furtive glances towards Grandpa Ernest. He cleared his throat slowly before pushing out the words that had caught there.

"It's up to Dan to apologise. And he should." Grandpa Ernest stared down the length of the table. "But I won't accept his behaviour – ever."

Grandma Mary looked mournfully at Lizzie's mother who shook her head slightly before dropping her gaze down to the half-eaten burger lying on her plate. There was the sound of cutlery scraping across plates as everyone turned back to their food. Joe began an explanation of how they would dig out the foundation for the new extension while Charlotte sighed and loaded her fork with another mouthful of coleslaw to listen to the discussion she had heard so many times already.

The twins grinned at her with, Lizzie thought, a hint of menace. She sat through the rest of the meal in a self-imposed isolation. It was only after they had eaten blackberry cobbler with a scoop of vanilla ice cream and Lisa and Laura were roasting marshmallows over the dying coals on the barbecue that Lizzie was able to relax from the tension caused by her question.

Lizzie was excused from the kitchen clean-up but could see the outline of her mother at the window as she washed the dishes and gossiped with the other women. She wondered if they were talking about Dan or had other topics to discuss.

The men sat looking out over the nearby fields, assessing how soon they would be ready for the team of combine harvesters to tackle the corn. Perhaps, they debated, there was one more crop of hay to be had from the southern edge of the farm. The end of the summer's work could now be seen on the horizon.

After a few minutes, Sam pushed back the remaining plates on the table and pulled out a deck of cards taken from their grandparents' games shelf. The edges of the cards were worn and they stuck together as he shuffled them.

"What'll we play?" he asked but before Lizzie could answer the twins took chairs on either side and shouted 'Cheat!' The afternoon dissolved into screams and accusations as all four of them tried to lie about what cards they were discarding from their hands in order to win the game.

Sam, of course, won the first round, but Lizzie began to spot the tells when he was lying. Laura was more likely to be honest , but Lisa challenged them on every turn to call her out, hoping that they would fall victim to her lie and have to draw more cards. By the third round, Lizzie's guesses were becoming more accurate and she forced the despondent twins to draw more cards from the deck while her own hand dwindled to a win with no cards.

The afternoon was nearly gone. The men were winding up their conversations and the women had packed up any leftovers to take home. Sam had just tried to sneak a lie back past his competitors when Lizzie caught the twitch of his eyebrow and called him out.   She was aching from laughing at the woeful look on his face when they heard a distant phone ringing from inside the house.   A couple minutes later, Grandma Mary came out the back door, her mouth drawn in a worried line.

"Jackie's started labour," she said. "She needs the hospital."

"Dan's job," Grandpa Ernest replied gruffly.

"You know he can't – he's banned from driving."

"Can't help," Grandpa Ernest said. "Got the milking to do."

"I'll take her then." Grandma Mary started for the house.

"Wait," Lizzie's mother called. "There's Simon as well. Who's going to look after him?"

"Guess I can look after my grandson!" Grandma Mary looked at her husband who turned his back as he folded up the chairs to take back inside.

Lizzie's mother shook her head. "It'll be easier if I drive them and take Lizzie. She can look after Simon while we settle Jackie at the hospital."

The Sunday afternoon suddenly disappeared and there were quick goodbyes. Sam and her father were dropped at home to start the evening chores, while Lizzie swapped to the front seat next to her mother for the drive to Dan's house. He was pacing across the porch waiting for them as they pulled up. He shouted into the darkness of the house and an expansive Jackie swayed into view. Dan helped her awkwardly down the steps before she stopped to breathe deeply as she held her belly. Lizzie could see the pain working across her face.

Simon peered through the screen door to see what his parents were doing. Lizzie ran up and stopped him before he could open it.

"You stay with him until I get back to take you home," her mother called to her as she helped Jackie into the front passenger seat.

Dan raced back to the house and grabbed a small suitcase waiting by the door. He stared at his son and then up at Lizzie.

"Be good for Lizzie," he said patting Simon's head. Then he was gone and Lizzie was left with the young boy looking at her with trusting wide eyes.

"You'd better show me where your toys are," she said closing the door and wrapping the comfort of the living room around her. Simon rushed to his toy box while Lizzie scanned the family photos sitting on the small bookcase. Dan and Jackie's wedding photo took centre place. She smiled remembering the cool spring day. They had shivered as they waited for the photographer to line up the family on the church steps for the picture.

Grandpa Ernest and Grandma Mary looked proud standing next to the newly married couple with their other children displayed around them. Sam was at the gangly stage of teenage growth. Johnny wore a handed down jacket from his brother which sat loosely on him with the sleeves engulfing his hands. The twins were in kindergarten and peered at the camera with cavernous smiles of missing teeth.

Simon was suddenly beside her running his favourite fire truck across her foot.

"Drink?" he asked.

They moved into the small kitchen and Lizzie settled Simon on a chair sitting at the table. She pulled the fridge door open to look for juice. She had thought Dan might have cans of beer cooling in the fridge for later. He was, after all, a drinker. But the only drinks were milk, juice and a few bottles of Coca Cola. She hoped that was a good sign.

Lizzie poured a small glass of orange juice for Simon and made a peanut butter and jelly sandwich cut into small pieces in case he was hungry. The chubby fingers and face were soon sticky and sweet and Lizzie sighed as she thought how she would have to scrub off the mess before they snuggled down on the sofa so she could read his books to him as they waited for her mother to return and take them home.

28 August 2018

    The apples in the bowl on the kitchen counter felt elastic and had pinpricks of brown spreading across their formally crisp surfaces. Elizabeth wondered if she could rescue them by making a pie, but the thought of turning on the oven for that long in the heat was overwhelming. She didn't know if Richard would be home for supper and the effort of cooking for just herself was too much. She put the dimpled apple back in the bowl, took a glass from the cupboard and filled it with orange juice from a carton in the refrigerator.

    Henry's letters were spread across the oak desk. She had been reading through the last ones for clues to how his life would develop. As their lives at university consumed their time, the letters had become more infrequent. Her surprise visit to Leeds created a mini tornado of correspondence in the spring of 1973 which quickly dissipated after causing emotional havoc.

    Elizabeth picked up a letter dated from the following March. The words were long and tired. Henry complained about the amount of studying he still had to do and the lack of time. He recited the essays to be written and the number of days until the Easter break. "I don't know how I will finish it all, but I will have to get it done somehow," he said, but he never asked what pressures she faced or mentioned being too busy to write at Christmas.

    She returned to the kitchen and set the glass beside the sink waiting to be washed. It would sit there until the next round of dishes when she would stand here and look out to the back yard as she cleaned the plates and wonder why she was there. Tomorrow would just repeat today. And the day after would be the same. She had tasted the fizz from the letters and hoped it would free a forgotten part of herself. But, now it had gone flat and she felt the weight of the everyday pressing down her shoulders and crushing her reserve of optimism.

Elizabeth sat down at the kitchen table and listlessly flicked through one of the catalogue brochures that came in the post whether or not she ordered from them. There were always so many promises that their products could clear your clutter or make your life easier. A better, more perfect, life always seemed just out of reach.

She didn't hear the front door open and was startled when Richard called out. Elizabeth hurried to the kitchen doorway just as he reached the desk covered in a patchwork of letters.

"What are you doing home?" she challenged.

Richard ignored the sharp tone in her voice while fingering the edge of an envelope covered in bright graphic lettering.

"What's all this?" he asked.

"Just some old letters," Elizabeth said dismissively.

Richard picked up the letter and peered at the postmark. "Hey, this is nearly 50 years old!" He turned it over and read the sender's name and address.

"So who's this Henry, then?" He looked up at Elizabeth, a shade of doubt crossing his eyes. "Boyfriend?"

"Just a pen pal I had when I was young."

"You never mentioned him."

"It was a long time ago," Elizabeth stalled. "I never thought it was important."

"That's a lot of letters," Richard said catching the lie. "Where've they been all this time? I don't remember seeing them before."

"They were at the farm. I found them when we were clearing out the house."

Richard loosened his tie and walked past her into the kitchen. He turned the tap to let the water run cold and filled a glass to drink. After the last swallow, he turned slowly back to her.

"So, you've had them for months, but never mentioned them?"

Elizabeth felt the sting of the question.

"If they weren't important," Richard continued, "why hide them?"

Elizabeth flailed for an answer. "It was private. Something from a long time ….."

"But I don't remember", Richard interrupted sharply, "in 37 years, you ever mentioning him before. Can't believe you'd be so secretive if it had been a girl."

Elizabeth felt a wave of embarrassment rising up her neck. Why had it mattered, she wondered, knowing that this should be a part of her past to leave behind. She couldn't explain the tug of that period of her life and instead shrugged slightly.

Richard walked back to the desk and picked up another of the letters.

"So he lived in Singapore?" he asked looking at the foreign stamps.

"When we started writing, he did," Elizabeth said quietly. "Later, he moved to England."

"That explains your sudden interest in that country, then," Richard rationalised. "Were you planning on looking him up?"

Elizabeth stood frozen in shame.

"Wait," Richard recalled, "you said you didn't go to London, but you went to England before we met. Was that to see him?"

Elizabeth nodded. "We were just friends, nothing more."

"But why keep it secret? That's what I don't understand."

Elizabeth wrapped her arms around herself in a hug. "It was just one of those 'what ifs'."

Richard looked at her questioningly.

"You know, what if you had made a different choice, what would have happened?"

"Like what if you hadn't married me?" Richard sounded bruised.

"No," Elizabeth rushed to re-assure, "that was the best decision I could have ever made." Suddenly, she recognised the truth in what she said. "This was just a fantasy from another time."

Richard sat down at the desk, picking through the envelopes.

"Are you sure?" he asked. "You've been so distant all summer. I felt like I couldn't reach through to you. Something was getting between us. Finally I know what."

"You think *I* was pushing you away?" Elizabeth held his gaze. "You were the one who was never here! So many nights *working*." She emphasized the last word with sarcasm. "How can you work so much when you're part-time?"

"I was about to tell you before I saw this," Richard swept his hand over the letters.

"What, that I've got competition?"

Richard looked perplexed.

"Who is she?"

"I have no idea what you are talking about."

"You must be spending your evenings somewhere and I can't believe it's all been work." Having blurted the words aloud, Elizabeth saw a real possibility in them. She had been angry with Richard for his absences, but until this moment had not felt betrayed. A thread of fear wrapped around her confidence.

"Are you seeing someone?" she asked.

"How you could think that," he answered. He held his head in his hands, running his fingers through the salt and pepper hair.

"If you have to ask that," he continued, "then you don't trust me and you may not believe me, whatever I say."

Elizabeth recoiled from the words. At no time during their marriage had she not trusted him, and this doubt was new and unexpected. She dug into its murkiness and tried to swipe away the allegations to find its heart. Lying at the base of her insecurities, she saw the doubt was aimed at herself. She was the one searching for something else. She was the one who was emotionally disloyal.

Richard stood and walked out of the room. She heard his steps cross the bedroom above as he changed out of his suit. The pipes hummed with the sound of water running to the shower and she wondered if he was cleaning off the work day or her unfounded accusations.

Elizabeth collapsed onto the desk chair, surveying the pile of letters. With a long swipe of her arm, she gathered them in and shuffled them into the box which she put into a drawer. If only, she thought, it was as easy to clear her mind.

She lifted her head and looked out to the back yard and garden, thinking how it looked when they moved in. It took years for the plants to grow into the vision she had had in her head, but that hadn't mattered because they had time. This was their forever home. She remembered the excitement they felt the first time they walked through the front door and knew as they turned to each other at exactly the same moment it was *their* home.

Baby Zoe stared at her from a photo waiting on the desk to be framed. Elizabeth smiled at the similarity to Kiera and the memory of holding her new born daughter flooded through her. It was just the three of them sitting in the hospital room and Elizabeth could not think of a more perfect moment in her life. At every good time and hard time, she knew she was part of a team. Friends joked that they were the three Musketeers and she had never questioned that they were all for one and one for all of them – until she found the letters and allowed a wisp of a memory to muddle her life. Were a few teenage yearnings anything against a long happy marriage, she challenged herself.

Richard appeared at the doorway, his wet hair slicked back against his skull making him appear more gaunt.

"Henry was my first crush," Elizabeth explained. "An impossible crush. Nothing would ever have come of it, but I needed him. I didn't have boyfriends. My best friend moved away and I didn't really fit in with the others. Henry meant a lot to me – even if he was a long way away."

Elizabeth paused as Richard settled into an armchair to listen.

"He was funny and really arty and spent hours writing these long letters to me. I guess I did the same back. I don't remember what I wrote. I'd probably be embarrassed if I read my letters now."

"But at some time you met?" Richard interjected.

"It was when I was a student in Paris." Elizabeth sighed. "I told Helen about the letters and she convinced me that this would be my one chance to meet him. We hitchhiked over at Easter break. Oh, don't tell Kiera. We were wet and tired and the most bedraggled pair you have ever seen when we showed up in Leeds at his door uninvited and unannounced.

"But, somehow, it felt like the most normal thing to have done. It was the most open and unguarded welcome I think I've ever had. Henry's sister Susan was there and they had friends come over and we spent the night talking and laughing. Somehow we all just seemed to click. We felt part of the same tribe, I guess."

"So why keep this secret?" Richard struck at the heart of the issue.

"It's hard to explain. It was very private to me. These letters are what I needed to get me through that period of my life. I wasn't getting on with the kids at school. Writing to Henry gave me hope I could be what I wanted to be."

"But that's the past," Richard argued, "not who you are now."

"It started me wanting more in my life. I wanted Henry, but I also wanted to see more in other parts of the world. I felt small and insignificant on the farm and Henry was so far away in a place that was very different."

Elizabeth stopped as she picked through the memories.

"Finding the letters stirred up those old longings and I ended up comparing it to where I am."

"What you mean," said Richard, " is that you aren't happy in the here and now?"

Elizabeth breathed in deeply. Explaining her feelings had focused and clarified them. The confusion of the past and the present separated into clear divisions within her life.

"Everything was good. Is good," she added for emphasis. She let the words dissolve the barrier of secrecy she had used.

She hesitated. "Unless I've driven you away?"

Richard got up from the chair and crossed the short distance to the desk. He bent over and wrapped his arms around her, filling in the rift that had come between them.

"Everything's good," he confirmed. "Except Jenny won't be happy."

"Who's Jenny?"

"She's the woman I've been seeing." Richard laughed.

"Invite her round," Elizabeth smiled, recognising the joke, "and I'll explain for you."

"Actually, she's the project manager on the job we just finished." Richard moved towards the kitchen. "I've been desperate to get this last job done, but it's been going on for weeks with one problem after another. I was beginning to think we'd never sort it out – that's the reason for all the late nights."

"When you say 'last job?' " Elizabeth queried.

"That was my surprise ." A broad grin broke out across his face. "I am now officially retired. So, there's time for all that travel you had in mind -- if you'll let me come with you."

She let the words soak in and found that the edginess she felt since finding the letters was gone. The past was not as important as the present and she and Richard had a lot of plans to make for that. She sat back and closed her eyes letting a slow smile push up the corners of her mouth. It was good to be home.

Later, as they sat at the kitchen table eating pasta and salad, Richard asked what she was going to do with the letters. She ate slowly, considering the question with each mouthful.

"Maybe burn them," she said finally. "They'll be gone then."

"Without regrets?"

"Yes, it's time to let go."

Richard reached for the bundle of mail that he brought in from the box earlier. He pulled out a brown envelope with a foreign stamp.

"I presume this ties in with Henry," he said handing it to her.

Elizabeth looked at the return address and gulped when she saw it was from the Leeds Registry Office. She looked sheepishly at her husband.

"It was a moment's madness," she said, opening the envelope.

A photocopied document slid out. She pulled back the fold of paper showing it was a certified copy of the original.

"What is it?" Richard asked.

Elizabeth handed over the paper. Richard scanned through it and laughed.

"What were you hoping for with this?" he asked.

"I don't really know," she admitted. "It was just an impulse I couldn't shake. Guess it's for the best."

"Yes," Richard said laying down the document headed Civil Partnership. "I think your hopes for any romantic future are truly over now. I hope Henry and his husband are very happy."

2 September 1968

"More, more, more." The high pitched voice into giggles.

Lizzie smiled as she entered kitchen and saw Simon sitting at the table. His small head barely cleared the table top even though he sat on two thick mail order catalogues. Sam was entertaining him with silly faces while they waited for breakfast. His expression was caught mid-contortion in transition to normal when he turned to Lizzie.

"He's had me up since 5.30," Sam complained.

As bedtime approached the evening before, Simon had been settled in Johnny's bed for the night when there was still no news of the baby's arrival. The excitement of sharing the room with his big cousin meant

Sam had to read five long stories before there was a hint of sleepiness from the two year old.

"Any news?" Lizzie asked.

"Got a sister!" Simon shouted. He bounced with happiness, almost propelling himself from the precarious catalogue seat. Sam grabbed him before he fell between the chairs.

"About 1 this morning, apparently," her mother said placing a bowl of scrambled eggs on the table. "Dan called. He needs a ride home."

"Timed his driving ban well, didn't he?" her father's voice was iced with cynicism. "You all right getting him?"

"Told him we'd have breakfast and then come in." Her mother buttered a slice of toast before cutting it in half to give a piece to the toddler. She spooned a small amount of egg into his plastic bowl and encouraged him to eat. "Simon can see his new sister."

"He won't be able to see Jackie." Her father spoke over the top of Simon's head.

"I know," Her mother reflected. "She probably won't feel like visitors much anyway to start. It's good she'll have a few days in the hospital to rest."

As always, the radio was playing the local station. The newscaster reported the new Democratic presidential candidate, Hubert Humphrey, would be taking part in the Labour Day parade in New York City. He was going to make civil rights a key part of his campaign. Meanwhile in Chicago, they were still recovering from the clashes between police and demonstrators at last week's Democratic Convention.

While Lizzie and her mother cleared the table and cleaned the dishes, her father settled into his favourite chair with the remains of yesterday's newspaper to enjoy the holiday. Simon sat on the dining room floor with an old multi storey parking garage that they had found tucked away in Sam and Johnny's closet, running his cars up the ramp and into their spaces.

Lizzie could hear thumps from upstairs as Sam filled boxes for his return to college. It was his last day at home and she wished she could spend more time with him. He wouldn't care, she told herself, as he was probably going to see his girlfriend as soon as he was done packing. She felt the family shrinking into smaller pieces.

Sam was still packing as they left for the hospital. Lizzie sat in the back of the car with Simon to make sure he sat quietly on the wide bench seat. She remembered how much she and her brothers had moved around in the car when they were little. There was always a fight over who had to sit in the middle and sometimes they traded seats during the journey. A couple of times Johnny had wedged himself on the ledge in the back window until Dad shouted that he couldn't see. Simon complained he couldn't see out and Lizzie let him climb into her lap so he could look out as the fields of tall corn blurred past.

The astringent waft of disinfectant hit them as the doors of the hospital opened. The hallways were bare and long. Simon jogged beside her as he tried to keep up with Lizzie who was reading the signs to the maternity unit. They found the corridor with the large window overlooking the new born babies. Lizzie picked up Simon as they scoured each tiny face searching for family features. Her mother pointed at a cot in the second row.

"I think that says 'Williams'", she said. She waved to a nurse inside the room and pointed at the baby.

The nurse rolled the cot forward so they could see the newest member of the family more clearly.

Simon lunged toward the glass and pressed his face against the window to see his sister better.

"They're going to have to wipe down that window or no one else is going to see through." Lizzie heard her grandmother's voice behind her.   Simon giggled happily.

"Give your grandma a kiss, Simon."

The boy squirmed in Lizzie's hold as Grandma Mary brushed his head.

"Hand him to me," Grandpa Ernest said reaching out for Simon.

Lizzie gratefully released the solid toddler.   They watched, mesmerised, at the cocoon of blankets as the small pink face twitched and grimaced in her sleep.

"Dad!" Dan called as he emerged from the doors to the maternity ward, expectant hope spreading across his face.

Grandpa Ernest turned away slightly without speaking.

"Have you seen her – our little Sandy?" Dan beamed down at his new daughter. "Isn't she beautiful?"

"She certainly is," Grandma Mary replied. "Can't wait to hold her."

"When Jackie's home," Dan promised, "you'll get plenty of chances."

A heavy pause lay over them, broken finally by Dan's excitement.

"What d'you think of her?"   His question was aimed at Grandpa Ernest's back.

Grandma Mary shook her head in warning.

"Dad," Dan persisted, "I'm glad you came."

Lizzie's mother spoke to avert another silence. "How's Jackie?"

"She's fine," Dan said but his eyes never left his father's back. "Dad, please say something."

Grandpa Ernest lowered Simon to the floor and adjusted his shirt before speaking.

"After the way you have behaved this summer, how do you expect me to speak to you? With all the damage that you've done to the families in town? That boy could have been killed. Long-time friends no longer speak to me. All because of you."

Lizzie glanced at Dan, the hope pressed out of his frame.

"Don't wait for me to forgive and forget." Grandpa Ernest gave one last look through the window to the newest family member. "I am here for your mother. Nothing will ever stop her from seeing her grandchildren."

With that Grandpa Ernest turned and walked away. Everyone stood frozen watching him until he turned the corner and they heard the elevator ping.

3 September 2018

The water was running in the shower when Elizabeth woke up. She stretched an arm out over the expanse of the king sized bed next to her and found it empty. There was muted conversation coming from the hallway as other hotel guests made their way to the breakfast buffet. She relaxed into the contented moment, savouring the temporary idleness

They had set out early Saturday morning on the cross country journey to Indiana as their inaugural adventure. Richard joked it was more a misadventure but it was a chance to roam as they chose and pick their own schedule. They headed across to the mountains and became tourists at Luray Caverns in the Appalachian Mountains, joining the last of the summer season visitors in hiking down into the depths of the caves. Memories of visiting with 6 year old Kiera hovered nearby making them laugh with happy nostalgia.

They had spent the night in Charleston, West Virginia, before travelling up to Fenton on Sunday to meet her brothers at an Italian restaurant for dinner. Julia joined Sam for this last visit to the farm, but JJ's wife, Cynthia, stayed home to run their hardware store while he was away. Elizabeth was used to their split lives. Running a store was as demanding and restrictive as farming had been for their father and it had always been difficult for both to be absent from the store at the same time. She wondered how often she would see either couple after the sale of the farm, as they were dispersed over the width of the country.

Richard came out of the bathroom, damp from the shower with just a towel wrapped around his waist. Elizabeth eyed the square line of his shoulders and felt a forgotten lust. When he smiled at her, she was catapulted back to when they met and the memory of their first kiss. His leanness had been filled in over the years and there was a bit of spread at his waist, but that only reminded Elizabeth of the many good years together.

He threw himself onto the space beside her and rolled onto his side to face her.

"Ready for breakfast?"

"Definitely," she said, "I'm feeling very hungry."

Richard stretched his arm out around her and drew her closer. She stroked the graying hairs on his chest and rubbed the scar from when he fell off the ladder while putting up Christmas lights. Her hands hovered over his skin, barely touching, but she felt an electrical charge crossing between them. She looked up at his face and saw he was watching her intently. She cupped his cheek and

angled his head so her lips could reach his. The fierceness
of his returning kiss fired the desire that had lain buried
under layers of familiarity. She wrapped her arms tightly
around his back, spreading her fingers to grasp the bare
skin, and echoed his hunger. Finally, breathless, they
leaned back from each other.

"I thought you wanted breakfast," Richard chided.

Elizabeth slowly smiled, her eyes fixated on the
lips that had pulled back from hers. Her voice was husky
with choked emotions.

"They'll only have cornflakes, anyway," she said
as her mouth neared his once again and her hand slid under
the hotel towel.

By the time they arrived at the farm, the field for
parking was filling up. She felt the protective presence of
Richard's hand at her back as they wound their way to the
auctioneer's table. She wanted to press herself into his
side the way the way young people in love cling to each
other, but knew the attention that would draw. Instead she
surveyed the hunched shoulders of her parents' lifelong
neighbours, settled in groups to share gossip and speculate
on what would be the final sale price. Couples stood in
individual spaces, separated by time, endurance, and some
disinterest. Richard's hand grazed hers and she looped her
little finger briefly around his to prolong the contact.

Wayne Jackson was the auctioneer and handled
most of the farm sales that happened in the county. He
had taken over the business from his father, who Elizabeth
remembered ran the auction of her grandparents' farm
when they retired.

They could hear the rapid rabble of numbers as a
distant auctioneer sold off the remaining farm equipment
sitting in the barn and sheds. Sam, Julia and JJ stood
waiting under the old hickory tree, apart from the cluster
of people, for the land sale to begin.

"Good turnout," Richard said as they joined them.

"Don't know how many bidders there are," Sam replied. "I think most are here to say goodbye or rummage through the house!"

"Someone will want the farm," a voice said behind her.

Lizzie turned to see the wide blue eyes of her cousin looking at her.

"Sandy!" Elizabeth took in the fading auburn hair and the start of lines at the corners of the mouth. "So good to see you. Is your mom here as well?"

Sandy shook her head. "No, she wasn't feeling very well today and thought it best to stay home. I am to give her a full report though."

"Happy Birthday," Elizabeth said.

Sam and JJ looked surprised.

"Don't you remember?" Elizabeth teased. "She's a Labour Day baby. It's easier to remember when it's on a holiday. And your 50th, Sandy. It's all landmark birthdays this year! Have you been celebrating?"

"I'm in a household of men," Sandy complained of her husband and three teenage sons. "They'd never organise anything and I just couldn't be bothered. Who wants to celebrate getting older anyway."

Elizabeth caught a movement in the corner of her eye. A large silver haired man wearing a baseball cap walked awkwardly towards them with a slight limp in his step. He paused when he saw Sandy and then addressed JJ.

"Been wondering if you'd get here," he said.

JJ looked him over slowly and a big grin broke over his face.

"Ray! You're still in town then?"

"Yep, nowhere to go." Ray O'Neill looked across at the house with sadness. "We were kids when I was last here."

"Yeah, I'm sorry that our parents fell out," JJ apologised.

Sandy fidgeted, rocking back from foot to foot.

"Not your fault," Ray said and turned to Sandy, "nor yours either."

"Felt like our whole family was at fault, sometimes," JJ admitted.

"When I got injured that summer, my mom needed someone to blame. We were worried about Fred. We didn't know where he was and then I got hurt. It was too much for her. My parents were having money problems and then there were the medical bills. I just knew they were arguing a lot 'cause they were scared."

"Ray," Elizabeth interjected, "I found one of your hospital bills in my dad's old desk. It was with some of my grandpa's things. Do you know why?"

"Your grandfather was really good to us. He paid the bill. Mom said it was guilt money, but I didn't think that."

"It was my dad's fault," Sandy said, "wasn't it?"

"He was driving the car," Ray replied. "And he shouldn't have been drinking, but you know something? Because of this leg, I never got drafted. It kinda protected me."

Elizabeth stood transfixed to hear the story of that summer from a different view.

"You know," Ray continued, "my mother never really got over losing Fred. It's hard, even now, and especially with the big funeral for John McCain all over the television this week. He knew what it was like being a prisoner of war, just like Fred did. But Fred came back so broken by being in the camp, he never recovered. That wasn't anyone's fault but Fred's – he joined up to go to Vietnam."

Sam straightened and spoke in a measured voice. "We heard about Fred. We were so happy for you when he came back."

"That was about my last year at college," JJ added.

"We couldn't believe it when he came home," Ray said softly. "But he was never the same. People didn't know what was really going on over there until much later. The things he must have seen…or done – we'll never know. Fred wouldn't talk about it. Just kept it inside and let it eat away at him. We couldn't get through to him. And when he killed himself, my mother just went to pieces as well."

"Oh, Ray," breathed Elizabeth unable to articulate the grief she felt.

"She's got dementia now which doesn't help. She keeps going back to that time and picking at the worst that happened and we can't stop her."

They stood in self-conscious silence unable to change or mitigate the years of pain. The auctioneer picked up his microphone and ran a test. The bubbles of gossip were broken and dispersed while people took their positions to view the day's main event. JJ led Ray to one side as they filled in the decades with the details of their spouses, children and jobs.

"I didn't know the O'Neills growing up," Sandy said.

"They used to be really good friends,' Elizabeth told her. 'I found a little diary Grandpa Ernest kept when he was young – he and Ray's grandad were good friends as kids and stayed friends when they got married. And my mom was very close to Ray's mother. But that all ended with the accident where Ray got hurt."

"Seems as though Dad did a lot of damage that summer."

"Well," Elizabeth agreed, "it was why Grandpa said he couldn't come to family gatherings."

"When I was little, I thought Dad just didn't want to go. Now I know better."

Wayne Jackson turned on the microphone and called everyone to the auction. It started slowly but as the bids increased, the pace sped up. With a swift pounding of the gavel, the property was sold. Elizabeth looked at her brothers through damp eyes: their bond with these acres was cut.

Richard slipped an arm around Elizabeth's shoulders in comfort for her sudden bereavement. Like an expected death, the reality was still a surprise. She looked at the house and the ghosted images of their childhood played through her mind. She thought she had removed them when they emptied the house, but now she saw they were connected to this space and would remain with the new owners.

A smiling couple in their 30s approached the auctioneer's table to complete forms and make arrangements to pay. Elizabeth saw their parents standing nearby and recognised the father as a boy who had been a couple of classes above her in school. They were local and they were farmers. She was pleased the farm would continue and not be divided up and sold for development.

The crowd shrank as people said their goodbyes and left. Finally, it was just the family and they opened the screen door to the house one last time. When Elizabeth stepped into the living room, it felt familiar but alien at the same time. It was stripped of all the possessions that had made it their home. The unnaturally empty rooms echoed their sadness.

"Another ending," Sandy said coming up behind Elizabeth to look at the open space.

"Even though none of us were going to live here, it's still hard to let it go."

"Don't suppose you'll be coming back so much in the future."

"Probably not," Elizabeth sighed running her hand down the bannister.

"I was wondering," Sandy said, "if you could come to supper tomorrow. Mom should be feeling better by then and I know she'd like to see you, especially as you may not come back for a long time."

Elizabeth glanced at Richard talking with Sam.

"We'd love to," she said, "but we've made arrangements to go see my old school friend, Anna, tomorrow. Haven't seen her for 50 years, so we have a fair bit of catching up to do."

"Sounds like it." Sandy seemed disappointed.

"We were best friends and then she moved away and I never heard from her." Elizabeth laughed. "I've got a lot of questions!"

"I imagine so," Sandy said. "I hope you get your answers. But don't forget to come and see us again."

They toured the hollow rooms and said goodbye before shutting the door and turning the key. The journey back to the hotel was muted by the weight of the memories that travelled with them.

Elizabeth was both excited and apprehensive the next morning. She stirred her cereal listlessly when they sat down for the hotel's breakfast, anxious about re-uniting with her old friend. Even the smell of the cinnamon rolls did not take away the unease.

"We might not have anything in common anymore," she grudgingly said to Richard when he questioned why she seemed nervous.

"Doesn't really matter," he replied. "It's only a short visit -- not like you are committing to the rest of your life."

"I guess not." The knot in Elizabeth's stomach unwound a little and she reached for a roll.

It was already warm as they loaded their suitcase into the car. Summer was stretching into September and the weatherman said it would get up to 92 degrees today. Elizabeth longed for the crisp days of autumn and hoped the temperature would drop, as predicted, by the end of the week. They rolled up the car windows and put on the air conditioning for the leisurely drive south. The freeway took them over the flat terrain, skirting Indianapolis and passing by the shopping malls of smaller towns.

The last leg of the trip took them through a small town perched on the bank of the Ohio River. Elizabeth watched the Satnav guide them into the centre and then on to a residential street of weathered houses. They pulled up to a neat brick-faced house with a large porch. The front door opened before they reached the steps leading to it.

The woman who emerged had short faded gray hair. She was trim but her figure had settled with time and rounded for comfort. Elizabeth searched her face and compared it to her memories. When the woman smiled, she saw the familiar mischief in the corners of her mouth along with the creases added over the years.

"Anna!"

"You've guessed correctly," Anna laughed. "It's good to see you after such a long time." She motioned them onto the chairs on the porch.

"This is just like our last summer," Elizabeth said, explaining to Richard. "We spent a lot of time swinging on the porch watching the world go by. Or at least as much as went through Clarksburg."

Anna brought out some cold drinks and freshly baked oatmeal cookies.

"I see you're keeping up the baking," Elizabeth commended.

"It's certainly comes in useful with the diner."

They relaxed into the chairs. Elizabeth introduced Richard and how they had met. Anna told how her husband, George, had died the previous year from bowel cancer, but without any lingering resentment in her voice.

"He was a good man," Anna said. "We set up the diner together and he was good with the children."

"How many do you have?" Elizabeth pulled out her wallet and produced a photo of Kiera holding Zoe. "I have one daughter and one granddaughter."

"They're beautiful," Anna said. "I've got a daughter and two sons. The youngest in our tribe is about three months from being born. I do love babies though, so I can't wait."

From inside the house, the phone started to ring. Anna tried to ignore it, but as it kept ringing, she looked apologetically at them as she stood up.

"Expecting a call on some legal matters," she told them. "Sorry."

Richard sipped his drink and Elizabeth scrambled in her handbag for something to fan her reddening face. The afternoon's heat was rising and there was little shade on the porch. A battered old Toyota pulled into the driveway. They watched as the driver manoeuvred her swollen belly past the steering wheel. Her long blonde hair shimmered in the sunshine. Elizabeth watched as she flicked back strands of hair the same way Anna used to do. The girl picked up two bags from the back seat and slammed the door shut.

"You must be Elizabeth," she said climbing the steps. "We've been excited to meet you after all this time." She put the bags on a small table next to Richard.

"I can't imagine why," Elizabeth replied. "You're working at the diner, is that right? Sorry, I don't know you name."

"Ellie." Her mouth turned into a copy of Anna's smile. "I am for the moment, until this one comes," she added holding a protective hand across her stomach.

"What about after? Are you going to continue working? Would it be hard for Anna to run the diner without you?"

"Oh, she'll have no problems," Ellie said. "I'm only part-time anyway."

Anna re-appeared in the doorway.

"I see you've met Ellie and our soon-to-be family member."

"I brought your order," Ellie said to Anna. "I'll be back after the shift."

Anna nodded to Elizabeth, "I ordered some of my diner's food for you to try."

Ellie turned to Elizabeth and Richard. "I hope to see you later," she said before rocking down the stairs back to the car.

"I see the hair got passed on," Elizabeth chided. "I was always jealous of your hair."

"It's only good when you're young," Anna replied, stroking her short hair. "As you can see."

"Ellie seemed glad to see us."

"That's cause I've always talked about living in Clarksburg and you and your family," Anna said. "It was a good time for me."

"But why didn't you keep in touch, then?" Elizabeth was baffled. "You knew where I was, but I never heard from you."

Anna shifted in her seat and studied her hands for a moment.

"I couldn't, not to begin with." Anna raised her head and stared out across the road. "It wasn't easy to move here. Dad didn't have a job for a long time and my parents were struggling."

Something clicked in Elizabeth's memory. In one of Henry's letters he had told her Anna had written to his friend after they moved and said her father couldn't get work.

"But you told me he had a new job when you moved," Elizabeth protested.

"It was my fault we had to move."

Anna hesitated. Elizabeth waited until Anna finally cut the silence.

"I was pregnant."

"What!" The revelation upset the summer Elizabeth remembered. "But you never told me."

"I couldn't."

"You were only 15."

"I was very aware of that. You are, when you're in high school and you have a baby daughter to look after." Anna smiled briefly. "I missed most of the fun part of high school. I couldn't afford to go to college. It wasn't like we planned at all."

"But Ellie isn't that old."

"Oh, no," Anna smiled. "Ellie's my granddaughter. I'm soon to be a great grandmother. That really makes you feel old."

At that moment, the door opened onto the porch and a middle aged woman stepped out. Her fading auburn hair framed the wide blue eyes that matched ones Elizabeth had seen the day before. A sharp sudden gasp propelled Elizabeth into coughing. Richard handed her a drink before glancing at the new arrival. His eyes widened.

Anna stood up. "Lizzie, I would like you to meet my daughter, Charlotte -- your cousin."

Charlotte stood awkwardly. "I've wanted to meet you for a long time," she said. "Sandy was never sure how you'd react."

Elizabeth felt the world was spinning.

"Sandy knew?"

Anna explained that when Dan was killed in the car crash, she and Charlotte had gone to the funeral where Charlotte met Sandy for the first time. Charlotte always knew who her father was and Dan supported them when he could.

"It was a shock to Sandy because she hadn't known," Charlotte said. "But then, we agreed it was great to finally have a sister – for both of us."

"But what about Jackie?" Elizabeth felt lost in a secret world she had not known existed. She remembered when she had heard about Dan's death. "My parents went to the funeral too."

Richard cupped his hand over hers for support. Elizabeth laced her fingers through his and squeezed tightly.

"This is why we had to move," Anna said sadly. "Your whole family knew. If we had stayed, the whole town would have known. My parents didn't think they could cope with that and your family would have been destroyed. It was easier to move and pretend my baby's dad was some teenager I wanted to get away from."

"But you were too young." Elizabeth struggled with the details. "Dan should have been charged."

"You know they were different times," Anna said. "And even with the Me Too campaign now, there's a lot that's pushed out of view. I was foolish. It was just once, but I didn't object and always felt it was my fault."

"I'm lost for words."

"It was hard," Anna continued, "but I got the best part. I got Charlotte and I will never consider that a mistake. And then later, I met George and he took me along with Charlotte and gave me two sons."

Charlotte pulled up a chair. No one spoke while Elizabeth became dizzy from the whirl of images circling inside her head. She sat blankly staring as cars passed in the road as she tried to recall glimpses of that summer.

"Your grandfather didn't want you kids to know," Anna said. "My parents were afraid I would tell you. It was just too many secrets to keep. So we came here."

"Mom always told me about the family. She didn't want to hide it from me." Charlotte smiled. "We'd see Grandma sometimes cause she loved her grandkids, but I never met Grandpa. He refused to have anything to do with the big 'secret'."

"And here I thought it was Dan's drinking that was the problem." Elizabeth gave a sad laugh.

"He drank quite a bit when he found out. He didn't cope well," Anna explained. "And then there was that accident. Your grandfather was furious."

"We saw Ray yesterday at the sale," Elizabeth recalled. "He thought the accident saved him from the draft."

"Sometimes," Charlotte smiled, "the mistakes bring you good things."

Richard was talking, but Elizabeth couldn't understand what he was saying as she tried to review her life in this new context. She noted the lies by omission that her parents had supported through most of her life. While one mystery had been explained, the decades-long artifice crushed the belief she held in her parents' and grandparents' integrity. The bedrock of her life had suddenly turned into sand and she thrashed around for something solid.

"I think the family is good at keeping secrets." She heard the tinge of sarcasm in Richard's voice.

Anna angled her head in a question.

"I only found out recently about Elizabeth's first love," Richard said. "And she'd kept his letters for 50 years!"

"It wasn't like that," Elizabeth protested but relented under Richard's piercing stare. "Well, maybe it was. Do you remember I had a pen pal from Singapore? I found his old letters when we cleared out the farmhouse."

"I remember those very colourful letters you got," Anna replied. "His friend wrote to me a few times, I think.

It was good to have someone to talk to who didn't know anything about me."

"I've been on kind of a nostalgia trip this summer, which is why I tried to find you." Elizabeth paused. "If you were in touch with my family, why didn't you contact me?"

"Knowing how much your parents tried to keep this quiet," Anna said, "I didn't think I could do it. It's really only Jackie's secret now and she's let Sandy and Charlotte get to know each other."

"I can't understand why she stayed with Dan," Elizabeth looked at Richard. "I don't think I'd ever trust again."

"She stayed because there was too much to lose. Not only did they have a new baby to worry about -- if they split up, everyone would want to know why." Anna leaned back in her chair. "Dan stopped drinking. Jackie said he promised never to betray her again and he helped out supporting Charlotte when he could."

Anna sighed. "But I don't think he was ever completely happy after that. He always felt the guilt and his parents virtually disowned him."

Elizabeth looked across the faces from Richard to Anna to Charlotte and saw a new history re-designing that distant summer. There were now undercurrents and eddies in what she had thought was the placid flow of their lives in a countryside where little happened. She thought that the sale of the farm was an ending of an era: she hadn't expected it to start another.

Printed in Great Britain
by Amazon